Helena forced herself to concentrate, and tried to ignore the faint, musky drift of Oscar's aftershave.

Clearing his throat, the solicitor continued, 'To my beloved great-nephew Oscar Iannis Theotokis I leave one half of the property known as Mulberry Court.' Adjusting his spectacles, he went on, 'And I also bequeath one half of the said property to Helena Kingston. All and everything to be shared equally between the two aforesaid parties.'

What had he just said? Immediately shocked beyond belief, Helena gasped and almost stood up. This isn't right, she thought wildly. Not Mulberry Court! There had to be some mistake!

If she'd been struck by something hurtling from outer space Helena couldn't have felt more stunned. There was complete silence for a few moments, then Helena pulled herself together and looked across at Oscar's stern profile, trying to stem the hot tide of feeling that was rippling through every nerve and fibre of her body.

Susanne James has enjoyed creative writing since childhood, completing her first—sadly unpublished—novel by the age of twelve. She has three grown-up children who were, and are, her pride and joy, and who all live happily in Oxfordshire with their families. She was always happy to put the needs of her family before her ambition to write seriously, although along the way some published articles for magazines and newspapers helped to keep the dream alive!

Susanne's big regret is that her beloved husband is no longer here to share the pleasure of her recent success. She now shares her life with Toffee, her young Cavalier King Charles spaniel, who decides when it's time to get up (early) and when a walk in the park is overdue!

Recent titles by the same author:

BUTTONED-UP SECRETARY, BRITISH BOSS
THE MASTER OF HIGHBRIDGE MANOR
THE BOSELLI BRIDE
THE PLAYBOY OF PENGARROTH HALL

Did you know these are also available as eBooks?
Visit www.millsandboon.co.uk

THE THEOTOKIS INHERITANCE

BY
SUSANNE JAMES

First published in Great Britain 2012
by Mills & Boon, an imprint of Harlequin (UK) Limited.
Harlequin (UK) Limited, Eton House, 18-24 Paradise Road,
Richmond, Surrey TW9 1SR

© Susanne James 2012

ISBN: 978 0 263 22682 9

THE THEOTOKIS
INHERITANCE

CHAPTER ONE

Just before three o'clock on a chilly April afternoon, Helena drew into the crowded car park of Dorchester solicitors Messrs Mayhew & Morrison, and glanced at her watch. She was five minutes early for her appointment—so she'd made good time on her journey from London.

As she'd left the motorway and joined the quieter country roads, the usual wave of nostalgia had run through Helena. Dorset was home territory—and she'd stayed away too long this time. In fact, she realized, she hadn't returned since her father's funeral four years ago.

Opening her bag, she took out the solicitor's letter and looked at it again. It merely confirmed the date of today's meeting when the will of the late Mrs Isobel Theotokis would be discussed. As she slipped the letter back into its envelope, Helena's eyes moistened briefly. Mrs Theotokis, who'd been her father's long-time employer, had obviously not forgotten Helena, nor her promise all those years ago that the precious porcelain figurines which had so fascinated the child would one day be hers.

Helena checked her appearance briefly in the car's

interior mirror. Her generously fringed, widely spaced blue eyes seemed to glitter in certain lights, and someone had once said that they belonged in a stained glass window. She had regular features and a small nose, and her milky skin, though typically English rose, reacted well to the sun's rays so that most summers she looked prettily tanned. And today she had chosen to wind her thick blonde hair up on top into a coiled knot.

She got out of the car and presented herself at the solicitor's office. The girl at the reception desk looked up and smiled.

'Ah, yes—Miss Kingston? Good afternoon.' She stood up and immediately led Helena towards an inner door. 'Mr Mayhew is waiting for you.'

As Helena was ushered inside, John Mayhew, the senior partner, stood up at once and came forward to greet her. He was a short, affable man with white bushy eyebrows and a moustache to match and he shook Helena's hand warmly.

'Thank you for making the trip, Helena,' he said kindly, and the girl's throat tightened briefly. She was known to John Mayhew because her father's modest affairs had also been handled by this firm, and the last time she'd been here was to finally settle everything up—and it hadn't taken long.

'Do take a seat,' the man said, adding, 'The other… interested party…has been delayed slightly. But he should be here any minute.'

Even as he spoke, the door opened and Helena turned her head, colour rising rapidly in her cheeks, leaving her breathless as the layers of her memory peeled away.

She was suddenly weightless, floating backwards in space…she was in free fall!

Oscar! Helena formed the name silently under her breath. Oscar…

This was Isobel's great-nephew whom Helena, three years his junior, had once worshipped…Oscar, who had initiated her into the first heady delights of romantic love. But that had been more than ten years ago…a lifetime away.

She forced herself to try and breathe normally as she looked up at him.

It was no surprise that he was still the most mind-numbingly handsome man she had ever seen—or would ever see—wearing his overt sensuality like a permanent badge of office. Helena gripped her hands together tightly. Why hadn't she thought that they might possibly meet again—and under these particular circumstances? But it had not crossed her mind, and she'd not been ready for it. But she met his gaze levelly as he looked down at her.

His glossy black hair was styled more formally than she remembered, but the chiselled, dark-skinned features, the expansive brow, the firm uncompromising mouth—that had closed over hers so many times—were still as enchanting as they had always been.

He was wearing a formal suit perfectly designed to do justice to his lean, powerful physique, but he had no tie on, his crisp white shirt partially open at the front, revealing the merest glimpse of dark bodily hair at the throat. Helena swallowed over a dry tongue as he looked down at her.

John Mayhew broke the few moments' silence. 'I

am sure you two must have met in the past,' he said, 'but let me introduce you again...'

Before he could go on, Oscar cut in, the familiar voice rich and evocative, with only a trace of his cruelly seductive native tongue. 'No need for that, John,' he said slowly. 'Helena and I know each other from when I used to visit my great-aunt at holiday times.' He paused, moving forward slightly, extending a strong brown hand in greeting. Then, 'How are you, *Heleena*?' And Helena's heart quickened. Because that had been Oscar's occasional, special pronunciation of her name. And hearing it again made her inner thighs tingle.

'I am well, thank you,' Helena responded coolly, half-standing to meet his outstretched hand. His long, sensitive fingers curled against her own, making her colour rise again. 'And you...Oscar?'

'Good, thank you,' he said briefly. He sat down on one of the big leather armchairs opposite John Mayhew's desk, and glanced briefly at Helena again. Pale, sometimes wistful, Helena had become a stunning, sophisticated female, exhibiting all of nature's attributes, he thought. She was wearing a dark blue, fine woollen suit and cream shirt and very high heeled shoes, her slender legs clad in sheer dark tights. As she looked across at him, her lips were slightly parted as if she was about to say something, but it was her eyes, those blue, blue eyes which had once known the touch of his lips, their charisma remained, unique, unforgettable. Oscar straightened up and turned his attention to the solicitor.

After all the usual polite greetings had been exchanged, John Mayhew opened a large file in front of him and began to read.

"'This is the last will and testament of Isabel Marina Theotokis of Mulberry Court in the county of Dorset...'" he read out, before proceeding to chant the detailed formalities. Watching him with her hands clasped in her lap, Helena was relieved that her heart rate was returning to something approaching normality. She wondered how many times in his life John Mayhew would have performed this task. Probably too many to count, she thought, hoping that the interview wouldn't last long and she could escape. The room was beginning to feel warm as afternoon sunlight filtered in through the high windows, and she automatically leaned forward, forcing herself to concentrate, and trying to ignore the faint musky drift of Oscar's aftershave.

Clearing his throat, the solicitor continued.

"'To my beloved great-nephew Oscar Ioannis Theotokis I leave one half of the property known as Mulberry Court in the county of Dorset together with all its contents, goods and chattels.'" Adjusting his spectacles, he went on, "And I also bequeath one half of the said property known as Mulberry Court with all its contents goods and chattels to my dear long-time friend Helena Kingston. All and everything to be shared equally between the two aforesaid parties.'"

What had he just said? Immediately shocked beyond belief, Helena gasped and almost stood up. This isn't right, she thought wildly. It was Isobel's coveted figurines in the library which she had promised would one day be Helena's…not the *house*! Not Mulberry Court! There had to be some mistake!

If she'd been struck by something hurtling from outer space Helena couldn't have felt more stunned… And she was not going to look across at Oscar be-cause—if this *was* true, and she quickly realized that it obviously had to be—she had virtually been given half his birthright! How on earth was he going to ac-cept that? That the daughter of his great-aunt's gardener was to receive such wealth! It was preposterous!

She forced herself to listen as the names of all the other beneficiaries were read out. There was a very long list, including a substantial sum of money for Louise, her housekeeper, and countless charities and local or-ganizations were included, but it was clear that the two main beneficiaries were Helena and Oscar.

'As in many cases, there are one or two details which have been added at the end,' the solicitor said. 'For your information, Mrs Theotokis has given some instruc-tions.' There was a long pause before he went on. 'She asks that Mulberry Court is not put up for sale until one year from the date of her death, and she asks that, if possible, prior consideration be given to a couple with a family.' He looked up. 'I happen to know that it was a matter of great regret to Isobel that she and Mr Theotokis never had children of their own.' He smiled. 'Maybe she is hoping that, one day, childish noise and chatter may echo through the rooms and grounds of Mulberry Court,' he said, 'and if it ever does,' he added kindly, 'I am quite sure that she will hear it all from her well-deserved place in heaven.'

Hearing those words made a painful lump form in

Helena's throat. Isobel Theotokis had been a gracious, kind and loving woman to everyone who'd crossed her path, and her final act of generosity to Helena was to actually give her part of the home she'd loved so much. What an incredible gift, an incredible honour! It was totally unbelievable, but in the short term how was it going to affect her? And just as important—what was it going to mean to Oscar? He wouldn't want to waste any time here—or anywhere else—that might distract him, even temporarily, from the famous Theotokis family business empire.

There was complete silence for a few moments, then Helena pulled herself together and looked across at Oscar's stern profile, trying to stem the hot tide of feeling that was rippling through every nerve and fibre of her body.

'Although I feel almost totally overwhelmed,' she began, trying to sound normal, 'it would be wrong of me not to say how very…grateful…I feel to have been remembered in such a way by Mrs Theotokis.' She hesitated, hoping she was saying all the right things. 'I shall, of course, do whatever is considered necessary to…well…to assist in any way I can,' she added, wondering what on earth anyone did when suddenly coming into a fortune that included a massive property full of treasures.

For the following few minutes Helena could barely concentrate on what the other two were saying, but presently, after some further formalities had been dealt with, the solicitor handed over two large bunches of keys, and Helena stared down at the set in her hand— her very own keys to Mulberry Court! And the way she was feeling at the moment, they might have been a ticking time bomb!

They all got to their feet, and as Helena looked up into Oscar's eyes—which were glittering like ice-cold granite—she couldn't begin to imagine what was going through his mind. The revelation that they were now joint owners of his great-aunt's home must have been as great a shock to him as to her, she thought—that she, Helena, was going to be playing an important part in his life, at least for the next year. Then, lifting her head, she thought—well, it wasn't her fault, and they were both going to have to make the best of whatever lay ahead.

After they'd been assured of Mayhew & Morrison's wish to be of further service when necessary, the two left the building together, and in the late afternoon sunshine stood outside briefly.

'Well—' Oscar shrugged and looked down at her with half-narrowed gaze. 'That was something of a surprise,' he said. *And that remark was something of an understatement*, Helena thought. *For both of them.* 'Still,' he went on, 'I'm sure we can come to some arrangement that suits us both.' The comment was casually made—as if he was merely referring to one of life's irritating necessities—and, before Helena could reply, he went on, 'I'll get someone to value the place in the first instance, give us some idea of value until we sell next year.' He shook his head briefly. 'Isobel requesting a delay is obviously going to hold us up. It would have been more convenient to have got things done and out of the way as soon as possible.'

Helena looked up at him, still feeling shattered, still

finding it hard to take all this in. Was she *really* here again with Oscar—about to embark on a serious business venture? Oscar, who'd been the true love of her life when she'd been on the cusp of womanhood. Oscar, who had shown her what desire, and being desired, meant? Their romantic meetings, many of them under the graceful branches of the willow tree beyond the orchard—their special willow tree—were indelibly imprinted in her memory, as was the way it had all ended so abruptly…as *he* had ended it so abruptly, with little explanation. After one of his visits, Oscar had simply walked away—and taken her heart with him. She bit her lip thoughtfully. Had their relationship ever crossed his mind since? she wondered. Had he ever felt anything at all—regret or remorse, or even sadness at losing something which had once been precious? Probably not, she thought realistically. She would only be one in a very long list of women who'd experienced his particular craft in the romantic stakes.

She swallowed hard, forcing herself to stop thinking along these lines. There was no point in digging up the past, even mentally, and she had quite enough on her mind—not counting today's revelation—to focus on. To sort out.

Looking up at Oscar, she realized that he hadn't expressed one word of appreciation that his great-aunt had remembered him in this way, but then, why would he? He was a bona fide member of the fabulously rich Theotokis dynasty, with vast worldwide business concerns. Mulberry Court and 'all its goods and chattels' would be no more than a blot of ink on Oscar's personal portfolio, and he was no doubt thinking that he could well do without this annoying interruption in his life, especially as it was going to include someone else—*her*! She lifted her chin.

'First of all, I think we need to discuss one or two things,' she said calmly. She paused. 'I happen to know that Isobel's personal belongings were tremendously important to her, and we should consider that point very carefully.' Mulberry Court was full of treasures—as well as those priceless figurines—which Isobel Theotokis had brought home from all the travelling she'd done in her life.

'Oh, valuers—experts in the trade—will deal with all the paintings and antiques. They'll ensure that everything's sold appropriately,' Oscar began. 'At least we can start to sort that out straight away.'

Helena frowned briefly. How typically masculine! He had no problem with Isobel's cherished belongings being handed over to complete strangers to 'deal' with, without a thought as to what everything had meant to the old lady. Well, Helena wasn't having that. She had spent so many happy hours at Mulberry Court when she'd been growing up—had almost been like the child Isobel had never had.

'I don't think that's a good idea,' she said. 'I think that that part of the equation should be our responsibility alone, without the input of strangers.'

Oscar raised his eyebrows—more in surprise that Helena had voiced her opinion than what she'd actually said. He shrugged.

'Well, yes, perhaps,' he said reluctantly, accepting for the first time that they both had to agree on everything before any action could be taken. 'But I'm afraid my time here is very limited. I'm due back in Greece by the end of the month, though I expect to be in the London office until then.' He paused. 'What about your own commitments?' he asked. 'I remember Isobel mentioning that you live and work in London.'

Helena nodded. 'I head the team at the Harcourt Employment Agency at the moment,' she said, 'but I have started looking for something else.' She bit her lip. So far, she'd found nothing which offered anything comparable with her present salary, nor the lovely mews cottage she was renting as part of the deal.

'You're not happy there?' Oscar asked briefly.

Helena paused before answering. 'It's just…just that I think it's time for a change,' she replied guardedly.

There was silence for a moment, then, 'I could come back this weekend—if you're free as well,' Oscar said. 'A couple of days should be enough to give us a clear picture of what has to be done.'

'As it happens I am free, and it would be a start,' Helena said, 'but it's bound to take some time, and we shouldn't rush things.' She paused. 'I intend to take the matter very seriously—and do my utmost for Isobel… in her memory,' she added.

She began walking across to where she'd parked her car, with Oscar following, and she opened her bag. 'In the meantime,' she said, 'if you think you need to contact me, here's my card.'

He glanced at it briefly, then withdrew his own from his wallet and handed it to her, and without even looking at it Helena slipped it into her bag.

'I must get back,' she said, glancing at her watch.

'The roads are going to be a lot busier than they were this morning.'

He held open her door for her, and as she got in she looked up at him through the open window, wondering if she should apologize for the situation they'd found themselves in—the situation that he'd been landed in. But before a single word had formed on her lips, Helena checked herself. She had nothing to say sorry for. Isobel Theotokis had every right to dispose of her property in whichever way she wanted.

'So—I'll come back down on Friday night,' she said, 'and that'll give us Saturday and Sunday to have a proper discussion and look over the house.' She switched on the engine. 'I'll book myself a room locally,' she added.

'I'll have to stay somewhere myself,' he said casually, 'so I'll see to it. I'll leave you a message to let you know the arrangements.'

'Oh… OK. Fine. Thanks,' Helena said, and with a brief wave of her hand she began driving slowly out of the car park, glancing in her rear-view mirror to see Oscar standing there, watching her go. She'd love to have been able to read his mind! So far he'd been cool, almost impassive, at their news, and once or twice she'd caught him staring at her with an inscrutable expression on his face. But it was good that there'd been no obvious sense of awkwardness between them, she thought, though there wasn't much doubt that he was wishing he was now the sole owner of Mulberry Court.

As she began her journey back to London, Helena felt mightily relieved to be alone with her thoughts. She, Helena Kingston, had just been left a fortune, and it was like winning a lottery she'd never entered. But was she prepared for such wealth? Her beloved father, a widower for many years, having lost his wife when Helena had been just ten, had left a very modest inheritance for his only child. Money which she had put aside for the day when she might need it for something special. And so far she never had, thanks to her successful career.

But quite apart from everything else—apart from even the amazing legacy she had just received—there was another problem she had to face: she and Oscar were going to have to spend time together again under totally bizarre circumstances. This wasn't ten years ago when they'd both been young and carefree and so in love, something which had been so important then, but which would be utterly embarrassing to even mention now. Did he remember any of it? she wondered. Did he remember all the time they'd spent walking, talking, kissing and enjoying spending time with each other? How could either of them pretend it had never happened? Helena made a face to herself. If he did remember any of it, he'd also have to remember how he'd dumped her—but then, he'd probably dumped so many other women since, she was just another note on whatever mental record he kept of his love life.

As Oscar got into his own car, his feelings were in turmoil. Because it had given his emotions a huge and undeniable jolt to see Helena today.

His handsome brow creased into a frown and his hands, tense on the steering wheel, became pale under his grip as he sat there for a few moments, deep in thought.

What had he done to her? What had he done to himself, to them both? Why had he allowed fate to rule their lives? Because when he had looked down into her wide, misty eyes, he was aware of his heart exploding into a million painful fragments of regret. The heart which had taken so long to heal had shattered again, renewing his sense of loss.

Over time, Oscar had managed to convince himself that he would probably never see Helena again. But he'd thought about her often enough, wondered who she'd married, how many beautiful children she might have. And while trying to concentrate on what was going on around them today, he'd automatically noted that there was no gold band on her ring finger and every male instinct he possessed had urged him to pull her up towards him, to enfold her, to taste her mouth again.

But he knew that would not have gone down very well. Why would she ever want him near her again? A nerve clenched in his strong jaw as his thoughts ran on.

Of course, it was not unexpected that he should be named as a beneficiary in his great-aunt's will because he was now the only member of his generation left— he'd never had siblings and his two cousins had been killed in a multiple car crash. But although he'd always known that Isobel had been very fond of Helena, the will *had* taken him by surprise, he admitted. Not that he cared a jot about having to share the value involved; that was irrelevant. Great wealth had never interested him in a personal sense. It was only the continuing success of the family firm that was important—ever since he'd realized that it was his destiny.

Destiny. Oscar's lip curled briefly. There was still one, more vital, personal expectation of him which he had so far not fulfilled. To find himself a suitable wife. And if his father—Georgios—had his wish, a wife from the rich Papadopoulos family, who had important financial ties with the Theotokis clan.

'It is about time you married and settled down, Oscar,' Giorgios frequently said. 'A good Greek wife would be a wonderful support, a wonderful investment! Would bless you with many children! There are those two beautiful daughters just waiting for you to make up your mind! Either of them would make you a happy man! What is your problem?'

The 'problem' was, Oscar knew he did not love either Allegra or Callidora Papadopoulos, desirable though they were. And no other woman, yet, had made him want to commit to lifelong love and loyalty. Because when he did find such a woman—if she existed—that was how it must be. For ever. And Oscar knew he would never view any wife as an 'investment'—as his father clearly did. Profit and loss were not part of the equation. Unconditional love was the only thing that mattered.

Now, straightening his shoulders, Oscar switched on the engine and prepared to drive away. For the foreseeable future he had a more immediate matter to resolve—the disposal of Mulberry Court and its contents. And it would be unavoidable that he and Helena would be spending a great deal of time together and that she was going to have to be consulted every step of the way.

* * *

Oscar had already decided which accommodation they'd be using and now, leaving Dorchester, he drove rapidly towards the Horseshoe Inn, an out-of-town up-market establishment a few miles away. It was small but well-appointed, and discreet—somewhere they could talk and get this business sorted without too many distractions. Vast hotels had never had any appeal for Oscar and he never used them if he could help it. And when in London he always used his private apartment, where he looked after himself and where this car—a favourite among the several others he owned—could be safely garaged.

Now, as the sleek grey Italian sports car took him swiftly to his destination, he remembered how confidently Helena had manoeuvred her own vehicle out of the overcrowded car park and he tilted one eyebrow thoughtfully. Her car was obviously not new, but in reasonable condition—and probably perfectly adequate for London use, he thought.

Although in recent years his aunt had often spoken of Helena—and always in glowing terms—he didn't really know anything about her career. His eyes narrowed slightly as a thought struck him. Perhaps he could pay her off, give her far and away more than the combined value of the house and all its assets and leave the business of disposing of everything to him? Surely it would be tidier all round if just one of them was involved. Wouldn't she find that far less hassle than having to spend time down here? Then he made a face to himself, discounting the thought almost at once. Helena—obviously very confident and self-assured—had given every indication that she intended being full-on in the whole assignment. He groaned inwardly. *Aunt Isobel*, he thought, *I always loved you, but why have you done this to me?*

CHAPTER TWO

AFTER a fairly tedious journey home, Helena made herself some toast and a mug of hot chocolate, then undressed and went into her bathroom for a shower. As the warm water began drenching her body and releasing the tension in her tired muscles, she kept reliving every moment of that incredible afternoon. Her life had changed! The world had changed! Well, it was certainly going to be different.

But Helena knew that all the formalities of the day, and the enormous significance of inheriting a fortune, were as nothing compared with the overpowering feelings she'd experienced at meeting Oscar again. Lifting her hair from the nape of her neck, she soaped her skin languidly, smoothing the sponge across her shoulders and down her arms, conscious that even thinking of him made her feel sensuous, dangerously sensitive. She remembered how her face had flamed crimson red as his brilliant dark eyes had bored into hers, how her pulse had raced, her tongue had dried as he'd stared down at her. She had wanted to look away, to escape from his entrapping gaze, but she hadn't been able to. She'd been transfixed by his nearness, helpless beneath his scrutiny, and she'd wanted to scream out in protest that she was no longer a young, inexperienced, naïve teenager! She'd grown up and moved far, far away from his sphere of influence! Her need for him had long since dissipated, had been replaced by all of life's other imperatives, like standing on her own two feet, holding down a good job that earned her enough money to survive in London's fast track world. And to make and keep friends, form relationships…to just *be*. Without *him*.

Yet now, it seemed, she was being forced to stand within his aura of light once again. But this time in a business capacity. How was she going to live through that?

Helena sighed as she reached for a towel, just thinking of business bringing her back down to earth and her present problems—the problems she'd been facing before today's revelations. Her problems with relationships.

Her split with Mark had happened two months ago—unexpectedly and painfully. And the trouble was that she kept bumping into him with the new 'love of his life', as he'd described her, both of them looking blissfully happy. That was bad enough, but then almost at once Simon Harcourt had started getting amorous towards her. Lately his attentions had become so annoying that Helena felt she would have no alternative but to leave the job, soon. Even if it did mean having to give up the cottage that went with it.

What she'd really like to do, Helena thought savagely, was to emigrate and get right away from everyone she knew in London and live in a completely different environment. Just until she got into calmer emotional waters.

Then, even as the unlikely thought of emigration crossed her mind, another amazing one struck her and she stared at her own reflection in the steamed-up mirror for a second. Could *Isobel* have given her an unexpected lifeline, an escape? Could such an impossible, fleeting idea work?

If she were to go and stay—well, live—just for a short time at Mulberry Court, she could reassess things and take stock of her situation. For the first time she would be in her very own home—well, partly her very own home—and find some peace to really recover from the emotional switchback she'd been riding lately. It would make it easy to give Simon her notice because she could tell him, quite truthfully, that her circumstances had changed and that for the next year she was needed in Dorset.

A wave of excitement swept over Helena as she considered all this. It really could be a temporary answer, she thought. She had enough money saved to pay for her immediate needs and anyway there was sure to be temping work she could find in Dorchester when she needed to.

She bit her lip thoughtfully. The big question was—what would Oscar think of her taking up residence, even temporary residence? Would he be agreeable to that? Wouldn't he think it opportunistic of her…or even inappropriate?

Presently, as she slipped into her nightdress, her mobile beeped, indicating a text message from Oscar: *'Horseshoe Inn bkd wk end. Meet Fri nt O.'*

Helena snapped the phone shut, wondering where he was now. What was he doing, and was he thinking about her at all? Was he feeling as confused about the afternoon's bombshell as she was? No, of course he wasn't, on either count, she decided at once. This would be a pretty insignificant affair to him, just another small and inconvenient detail in his important life which had to be sorted out. And everything in his attitude towards her had suggested that she, Helena Kingston, was merely part of that unwelcome inconvenience.

She slid gratefully into bed and pulled the duvet up around her shoulders, wondering whether she'd ever be able to get any sleep. She wished she had someone close that she could share her news with, a brother or a sister—it was far too late to ring her best friend, Anna. But still, she was used to steering her own way through life's sometimes turbulent waters without anyone's hand to hold on to. And she was certainly not going to let this particular tsunami sweep her under the waves.

Snuggling down, she tried to shut everything from her mind, to calm herself into believing that it would all seem straightforward in the morning. But how could it? Because behind her closed lids all she could see were Oscar's intense black eyes in their pools of startling white, gazing at her with that heart-stopping expression that had always sent shivers down her spine.

On Friday evening, Helena had no trouble in finding the Horseshoe Inn, though it was unknown to her. Situated on a private road and nestling amongst trees, the Grade II listed building backed on to open country, and after her long drive it looked like heaven.

Inside, the tall, bearded man standing in the small reception area by the crowded bar smiled at her enquiringly. 'Hi there,' he said. 'I'm Adam—can I help?'

'I believe accommodation has been booked for me for a couple of nights,' Helena said. 'I'm Helena Kingston.'

'Of course—yes.' The man glanced at the huge calendar in front of him. 'Room numbers two and five have been allocated, one for Mr Theotokis and one for yourself,' he said, smiling again. He paused. 'Would you like something to drink before I show you to your room? The chef's on duty until midnight if you'd like a meal,' he added.

Immediately, Helena felt completely at ease. The inn had a sophisticated air, yet was welcoming and reassuring, its ambience the sort she imagined Oscar would approve of—though what his opinions, likes and dislikes were she actually had no idea of at all. Not now, not any more. But, hopefully, they might have just enough in their shared pasts to make this unlooked for alliance reasonably pleasant. Helena certainly hoped so, even though his reaction to the news had been slightly ambivalent.

'I'd love a pot of tea in about ten minutes, and perhaps a sandwich?' Helena said, glancing over to the lively-looking restaurant area at the far end. She picked up the small case she'd brought with her, then hesitated. 'Is Mr Theotokis about?'

'Haven't seen him—and he hasn't booked in yet,' Adam said, taking a key from one of the pegs on the wall. 'Let me show you the way,' he said, taking Helena's case from her.

Her charmingly rustic bedroom with every conceivable mod con was going to suit her very well, Helena thought as she looked around her. She'd be quite happy to stay here for a couple of nights. Sitting on the edge of the huge double bed for a moment, she glanced at her watch. It was getting late and she'd imagined Oscar to have been here by now, and she wasn't sure what to do next. Would he expect her to wait around for him until he turned up, or could she go to bed after she'd had her tea?

At that exact moment her mobile rang. It was Oscar. 'Helena, I'm sorry to be this late,' he said. Then, 'I take it you found the place OK?'

'I did, and my room is excellent—thanks.'

There was a pause. 'I'm not far away, so I should arrive in twenty minutes or so.'

'Shall I... Would you like me to order something for you?' Helena asked. 'I'm told the chef's still on duty.'

'You can order me a whisky—but nothing to eat, thanks,' Oscar said, and without another word he rang off.

By the time he arrived almost half an hour later, Helena had eaten the sandwiches she'd ordered for herself, and was sitting in a quiet corner of the still busy bar with her glass of wine and Oscar's whisky already on the table. He came straight over and sat down opposite her.

'Hi,' he said briefly, then picked up his glass and took a generous swallow. '*You* obviously got here with no difficulty,' he said, sitting down, and feeling fleetingly pleased to be with someone he knew—or knew once. And she was looking good—amazing, in fact—in her jeans and striped sweater, her hair tied back in a long ponytail.

Helena couldn't help noting the dark expression on his features, and an uncomfortable chill ran through her. He was obviously thoroughly annoyed at being so late, she thought—or maybe he wasn't appreciating having to be here at all—with her. Helena's spirits sank at the thought of what lay ahead of them, of how he might view everything to do with their shared legacy. And, now that he'd had time to mull it over, how he was viewing her significant presence in the whole affair. Was he going to expect her to meekly see his point of view—to kowtow just because of who he was? And would she ever have the nerve to put her suggestion to him about staying at the house? He certainly didn't seem in a particularly positive mood at the moment, she thought.

'Anyway, it's rather late for us to discuss anything tonight,' he said briefly. 'So we'll have an early breakfast in the morning, then spend the rest of the day at Mulberry Court and catalogue all the items that need disposing of.' He took another drink. 'The quicker we make a start, the better.'

Helena finished her wine and picked up her bag. 'I'm aware that you have a very busy life, Oscar,' she said firmly, 'but...' She paused. 'I would really like to spend some time just looking around Isobel's home, revisiting something of my past, perhaps,' she said. 'I knew Mulberry Court so well when I was growing up, but it is such a long time since I was there—I wasn't even able to make the funeral—which upset me a lot. And Isobel's death was so sudden—so totally unexpected.' She paused.

'Yes, I thought you'd been forgotten,' Oscar said, 'that your name had somehow been omitted from the long list of my aunt's friends and acquaintances who would have been informed of her death.'

'No, I wasn't forgotten—and I did explain later, with my apologies,' Helena said carefully. 'I was actually ill in bed with a horrendous attack of flu,' she added, surprised that her attendance at what would have been a very crowded occasion had been missed by anyone— especially Isobel's ambitious great-nephew. She stood up.

'Well, then, I'll see you in the morning,' she said, and Oscar stood as well, looking down at her briefly.

'Yes, and tomorrow you can have your little trip down memory lane,' he said obliquely.

After she'd gone, Oscar bought himself another whisky and sat back down, relieved that the golden liquid was beginning to calm him, bringing him back to normal. The reason behind his lateness had been an accident that had shaken him up quite badly. In all the countless hours of driving he'd done, he'd never been caught up in anything like it—and he hoped he never would again. One of the first on the scene, and having to rescue two young kids from the back of a car that had seemed ready to burst into flames, had been a shattering experience. But the emergency services had arrived in an impressively short time and had been fulsome in their praise of Oscar's quick thinking—which, when he thought about it now, had been purely instinctive. He drank quickly again. It was a miracle that no one had been killed or badly hurt, though the young mother who'd been driving had clearly been in deep shock. Thank God he'd been there at just the right moment to be of some use.

After a while, his thoughts turned to his reasons for being here. In the few days which had elapsed since the reading of the will, he'd had time to think things over and had to accept that its contents—and instructions—were hardly Helena's fault. But one thing was certain—it was going to be a major inconvenience for both of them. Though, from what she had said just now, she was going to take her time. Well, if there was too much procrastination he'd have to hurry her up a bit, he decided.

He fingered his glass thoughtfully, that other idea occurring to him again. Could he get her to agree to sell him her share straight away? She might be glad of some quick money—living in London was expensive, and she could certainly do with a new car.

He drained his glass and went over to the bar for the key to his room. Adam looked up and smiled. 'Everything all right, Mr Theotokis?' he asked.

'I certainly hope it's going to be,' Oscar said enigmatically.

'No, no, *no*! You can't do this to me…it isn't fair! You *shan't* have them…you can have the house, you can have everything…but these are mine! Isobel promised!' And then a low, pitiful scream followed as the figurines fell to the floor and shattered into a thousand pieces.

Helena sat bolt upright in bed, putting her hand to her

mouth. Had she screamed out loud just then—had any-one heard her? That was one of the most awful, vivid dreams she'd ever had in her life. But this dream—this nightmare—had been so strong it had actually felt physical. She had felt Oscar's hands holding hers in an iron grip as they'd both struggled for possession of the beautiful ornaments. Pushing and pulling each other like demented creatures. But Helena had been no match for his masculine strength and with that cry of despair she had released her hold and watched her precious figurines destroyed before her eyes.

As the early dawn light filtered in through the slightly parted curtains at the window, Helena al-lowed herself a shaky smile as she waited for her heart rate to return to normal. Thank goodness for dreams, she thought, because that was all they were—mythi-cal wanderings of a half-awake mind. Her figurines were not smashed, they were still safely in their place at Mulberry Court, but could her dream have been a warning? she wondered. A warning to stand her ground with Isobel's nephew and not let herself be intimidated by the fact that he was a true blood relative and she a complete outsider?

Oscar had decided that they should start the day early, and Helena made her way downstairs to the restaurant for breakfast as early as possible.

He was already seated reading a morning paper, a large cafetière of coffee in front of him, and he stood up as Helena came in and glanced down at her. She was wearing slimline black trousers and a pale blue shirt, her hair tied back away from her face, which was devoid of make-up. She looked rather wan today, he thought, and for the merest second he saw again the lovely, innocent girl of long ago. He pulled out a chair for her to sit down.

'I'm impressed,' he said. Then, 'I didn't expect to see you for at least another hour.'

Helena shot him a look as she took her seat. 'I'm used to getting up early,' she said. She wasn't going to tell him that it was the horrible dream she'd had which had woken her at dawn.

Declining Oscar's invitation to share his coffee, Helena decided to order a pot of tea for herself, feeling very thankful that he, too, seemed to need little to eat. She had never been a breakfast person.

Later, driving rapidly in Oscar's car, they arrived at Mulberry Court and as they made their way along the broad, curved drive, Helena felt her stomach churn. This was now her house—partly her very own property. The much loved building she'd privately thought of as home all those years ago was legally hers! She still felt it too incredible to believe as she sat with her hands clasped in her lap, looking around her.

There, to one side, and out of sight of the main entrance, were the two semi-detached staff cottages, one each for the housekeeper and the gardener, and Helena turned her head to gaze back as they went past. After her mother had died, Helena and her father had come from their rented house in Dorchester to live in the gardener's cottage and for the following eight years, until she'd gone to university, she had lived what she now thought of as a charmed life, roaming free in the wonderful Dorset countryside and the extensive grounds of Mulberry Court, where her father had been the full-time gardener and general factotum. Louise, a local woman, had been Isobel's housekeeper and cook, and Helena would frequently drop in next door to enjoy her company—and share her wonderful home-made cakes.

As for Paul Theotokis, Isobel's husband, Helena had barely seen him at all. He had been a rather shadowy figure, constantly away looking after his business interests, but when Helena was about thirteen Paul had died suddenly, and the impressionable child had been amazed at the extravagant funeral arrangements and the hundreds of people who'd attended. Huge, glistening cars arriving, one after the other.

'Who lives in our…I mean…who lives in the gardener's cottage now?' Helena asked curiously.

Oscar glanced across at her. 'Benjamin. He joined the "firm", as my aunt liked to call it, a month or so after your father died,' he said shortly.

'And Louise? I know she's still here, isn't she?'

'She is. She's been keeping everything ticking over until…well, until the future becomes clearer,' Oscar said. 'But she's having a few days away in Durham with a cousin at the moment, I believe,' he added.

Poor Louise, Helena thought. Mulberry Court—and her little cottage—had been her home for so many years. Now there was the prospect of no home, and no employment, either.

Oscar drew the car slowly to a halt outside the entrance door to Mulberry Court, and they both got out and went into the house. And as soon as she stepped over the threshold, the smell of the place filled Helena with a warm rush of welcome. She took a deep breath, feeling almost faint for a second as a wave of nostalgia rippled through her.

'It's been such a long time,' she said quietly. 'Although Isobel very kindly arranged a small reception here for my father's funeral, it was held in the conservatory...and, anyway, I was so...distraught...I hardly knew where I was at the time.'

Oscar gave her a sidelong glance. 'I haven't been here myself much, either,' he admitted. 'There just never seems to be the time...or a suitable opportunity.'

Together, and not saying much, they wandered through the rooms on the ground floor, Oscar making notes as they went, though Helena didn't bother to follow suit. To her this was all so familiar, and little seemed to have changed, she noticed happily.

The glistening, well appointed kitchen was exactly as she knew it would be—the Aga still comfortingly warm and, in the dining room next door, the huge polished rosewood table was graced by the customary massive fresh flower arrangement in its centre. Helena smiled inwardly. Louise had obviously been determined that standards wouldn't be allowed to drop just because Isobel was no longer there.

The main sitting room leading into the conservatory was still furnished exactly the same, though the heavy ivory-coloured curtains at the full-length windows were new, she noted. The smaller occasional room next door was where Helena and Isobel had spent many evenings together playing Scrabble or watching television.

Further along was the library, which had always been Helena's favourite place, and now, as they went inside, she was stupidly relieved to see that her figurines were still there in their usual softly lit alcove.

But dominating the room on the opposite wall was the amazing gold-framed portrait of Isobel, and Helena had to put her hand over her mouth to stop her lips from trembling.

The painting was so touchingly real that it felt as if Isobel might get up from the chair she was seated in and step forward to greet the two of them in the room. She was shown wearing a soft, loosely fitting dress in a delicate shade of pink, her luxuriant silver hair elegantly coiffed on top, her large grey eyes smiling that gentle smile that Helena knew so well.

As with the other rooms, every available space was taken up to display all the ornaments to best effect and, as they turned to go, Oscar clicked his tongue, looking back briefly.

'My aunt was some collector,' he remarked obliquely. He refused to acquire much for his own homes, preferring to keep his space empty and clutter-free—much like his life.

'Yes—but there are collectors, and collectors,' Helena said, immediately on the defensive. 'Every single thing here is exactly right for its situation. Isobel had an eye for such things and she had wonderful taste—and it shows.' She paused, her head on one side. 'I don't know what you intend…I mean…I don't know what your opinion is, but I think it's best if everything is left exactly as it is for the time being—until after the sale of the house, I mean. I don't think we should move a thing. After all, any prospective buyer is going to be far more impressed when viewing a property that looks lived-in…loved…cared for.' She looked up at Oscar earnestly. 'Once everything's gone, the house will be just an empty shell. Lifeless.' The fact was, she admitted, she couldn't bear to see Isobel's beloved home broken up and sold off in bits and pieces, even though it was inevitable one day. To Helena, it would seem like the ultimate betrayal.

A nerve pulsed in Oscar's neck as he looked down at her, and he was aware of a certain hunger he hadn't felt for a very long time.

'We'll have to think about that,' he said, averting his gaze. Then, 'By the way, as far as I'm concerned, you're welcome to have anything you want… Take it now.' He paused. 'I don't need any of this,' he added.

Helena looked up at him seriously. No, I don't expect you do need anything, she thought. And did she, Helena, *need* anything? Despite her prospective inheritance, she could never envisage a time when she'd eventually settle somewhere which would happily house such wealth.

'I don't want to think about what I want, or don't want or need,' she said coolly. 'Not now. Not yet.' She paused, her gaze lingering on the figurines for a second. 'Only those over there—the shepherd and shepherdess—they are the only things that I would love to have.'

'Feel free to take them, but it'll all have to go eventually,' Oscar said firmly. 'Putting off the inevitable is just procrastination.' And procrastination hinders progress, he thought. He avoided procrastination wherever possible.

Presently, Helena followed Oscar up the wide staircase to the first floor. Immediately ahead, there were the four bedrooms, and around the corner to the next wing were two more, all with en suite bathrooms, the long windows on this generous landing lighting up the pattern on the richly carpeted floor.

Helena caught her breath as her memories kept flooding in. This was the first time in over nine years that she had been upstairs at Mulberry Court and she had to resist the temptation to run along and throw open the door of the room at the far end which had been 'hers'—the one in which she had stayed on the few occasions that her father had had to go away.

'Isobel had so many friends…I remember she was always entertaining, always having people to stay. These rooms were never empty for long,' Helena said, adding, 'I stayed here once or twice.'

'And…this was my room,' Oscar remarked, throwing open the door to the one they'd come to. He paused, looking around him. 'I used to enjoy my visits,' he added, and Helena's heart missed a beat. Could he actually have forgotten what his visits had meant to *her*—to both of them? Had he completely obliterated those times from his memory? Had they meant nothing?

After a few more minutes they went outside to wander through the grounds. The kitchen garden at the back was still flourishing and well-kept, Helena noticed, trying not to feel too sad that someone else was now in charge there. Though Benjamin didn't seem to be around today.

Nothing had changed outside, either, she thought, her eye drawn towards the secluded wooded path that led to their willow tree and, even after all this time,

Helena could feel her senses swim at the memory of the intoxicating moments she and Oscar had experienced together. Yet they were walking here now as if none of it had ever happened. As if they were two strangers in a foreign place…

Without her realizing it, Oscar had been looking down at her as they walked, his eyes following her gaze as she'd been reminiscing, and abruptly, as if he'd had enough of all this, he stopped and turned.

'I need to get back to the Inn,' he said briefly. 'I want to check my emails, and I'm expecting an important phone call.' He glanced at his watch. 'Anyway, it's gone one o'clock—you're probably ready for some lunch, aren't you?'

To her surprise, Helena wasn't feeling at all hungry, despite having had no breakfast. But another of Adam's delicious sandwiches suddenly seemed attractive.

'OK,' she said casually as they walked towards the car. 'And, actually, perhaps I ought to phone my boss. He hasn't been in the office for a few days, but I know he's back this weekend. Perhaps there's something he needs to tell me before Monday morning.'

As they drove back to the Horseshoe, something made Oscar decide to try his luck. He'd been thinking about it for the last hour or more, but he knew he'd have to pick his words carefully.

'Look, if it would be any help to you, Helena…I'd be more than happy for us to get a true valuation of Mulberry Court, the contents, everything,' he said carefully, 'and, allowing for inflation, to pay you a very generous half of the total, now. It would relieve you of all responsibility, and you've said you don't want anything for yourself…other than those figurines.' He turned to glance at her as she sat beside him impassively. 'It would save you a great deal of trouble…'

There was complete silence from Helena, and he went on, 'Of course, the sale can't proceed for a year, as we both know, but if you agree, at least one of us will be spared considerable interruption to our life. John Mayhew would sort out the transaction for us, I'm sure,' he added.

He drew into the car park and looked across at Helena, noting her flushed features.

'You've forgotten what I said, Oscar,' she said, staring straight ahead. 'I've already told you—I want to be able to play my part in making sure that we deal sensitively with all the material possessions which Isobel held dear.'

Now she did look at him, her eyes almost crackling with distaste. She knew what his game was—he wanted her out of the way! For his own convenience, not hers. She was an unnecessary encumbrance! Although he may have cared for her once, he didn't care about her now and he didn't care about Isobel's lovely things, either, which he'd make sure went to the highest bidder.

She opened her door, then looked back at him squarely.

'I am grateful for your concern at the "interruption" to my busy life,' she said, 'but…thanks, but no thanks, Oscar. Mulberry Court and I have a very long way to go before we're through.' And with that she got out of the car and walked swiftly towards the entrance to the Inn.

* * *

Back in his room, Oscar took his laptop from the wardrobe and threw it down on the bed, admitting to feeling unusually distracted. Exploring Mulberry Court this morning had ruffled his memories more than he'd expected and he'd felt his aunt's presence in every corner. He knew he had always felt closer to her than to his own parents, and her wise gaze as she'd looked down at him from that portrait had unnerved him slightly.

He shrugged. Anyway, he'd probably blown any chance of Helena agreeing to his perhaps unrealistic proposal. It had obviously been the wrong moment to have mentioned it, he thought. If ever there was to be a right one. He remembered enough about her to know that she had a mind of her own, and would not easily be persuaded into making decisions she might later regret.

But what to do with the house and its contents was a totally insignificant matter compared with the far more vital one to be handled, he thought. Because he had the distinct feeling that he'd been awakened from a hundred-year sleep and by the most desirable woman he'd ever known. Or was ever likely to know. But had he woken up in time?

CHAPTER THREE

TRYING to subdue her somewhat ruffled feelings, Helena went into her bathroom to wash her hands and put a brush through her hair.

The morning had been a rather emotional experience, she thought. At certain points it had seemed to her as if she and Oscar were trespassing, which was obviously silly because Mulberry Court was legally theirs. But Isobel's presence had seemed to follow them as they'd wandered through her home, and it seemed wrong to Helena that she hadn't been there as well.

But what was really getting to her now was Oscar's proposal that she should wash her hands of their present situation and leave him to it. Even if it would obviously mean that straight away a very considerable amount of money would come her way. She sighed briefly. He wouldn't have the sensitivity to understand her feelings—the look on his face had said everything. But she felt, acutely, that Isobel had left this assignment to the pair of them, to be handled with dignity, obviously thinking that two heads were better than one.

Helena frowned as she dwelt on all this. Perhaps she was being mean, not giving Oscar the benefit of the doubt. Perhaps he really *did* have her interests at heart.

Then she shook her head, responding to that thought. No, this was all about him, wanting to go it alone without the handicap of someone else possibly having an opinion that didn't match his. He was, after all, a cut-throat businessman—he had to be, surely, as the head of the Theotokis dynasty? Sentiment didn't come into it because everyone knew that there was no room for sentiment in business.

With her head beginning to throb with all these teeming thoughts, Helena decided that for the moment she'd had enough. Taking her mobile from her bag, she dialled his number.

'Oscar, I've developed rather a bad headache,' she said calmly. 'So I'm going to have a lie down. Perhaps we can continue our…discussions…later. At supper?'

There was barely a pause as he responded snappily—she'd obviously interrupted something. 'Fine. I'll book a table downstairs for eight.' And, after a moment, 'If you think you'll have recovered by then.'

Helena could imagine him raising his eyes impatiently at what she'd just said. Then she sighed. She didn't usually have negative thoughts about people, about anyone, but somehow, she and Oscar… It had to be the disparity in their positions which had ignited the latent inferiority complex which she occasionally had to battle with, she thought. Well, thanks to Isobel, for the moment she was now exactly on a par with him. There was no need for her to feel that he had any advantage over her at all, and she must keep reminding herself of that. For one year, they were to be partners.

'Oh, I'll be fine by then,' she reassured him. 'I'll see you at eight.' And with that she rang off. Anyway, she thought, he wouldn't be sorry to have some time to concentrate on far more important things.

As he drank his glass of whisky in the bar, Oscar had to accept that the morning hadn't gone as he'd expected. He'd fondly imagined that he and Helena could have had a straightforward discussion about his aunt's possessions—to make a list of what they wanted to take away with them, wanted to sell, to at least have made a beginning. He'd fully expected Helena to want some of the contents of Mulberry Court for herself, maybe a picture or two, or a small chair or some books, things that would easily fit into her car to take away. Arrangements could be made for anything else she might fancy to be delivered to her place later. But apparently she didn't wish for anything at all except those ornaments, and she'd made it clear where her instincts lay—to leave it all in situ.

Helena was just lying on the bed reading her book and sipping the last of her coffee when her mobile rang. As she answered it, Simon Harcourt's voice met her ears and she frowned slightly. 'Oh—hello, Simon,' she began, then listened for several minutes while he explained the reason for his call.

Interrupting at last, Helena said, 'Actually, Simon, I won't be available to come to the conference with you that weekend because…I'm afraid I shall actually be giving you my notice on Monday,' and before he could say anything, she went on quickly, 'I've learned that I've just inherited a property in the country, and it's not a straightforward matter, so I need to leave London almost at once.' She swallowed, hard. Well, she'd burned her boats as far as Simon was concerned. Where she stood with Oscar was another matter!

Helena slipped into her simple knee-length three-quarter-sleeve aubergine dress—which she'd decided at the last moment to bring with her—and glanced at herself in the mirror. The garment was still a favourite item in her wardrobe, and whenever she wore it she always made a point of sweeping her hair up on top, which she felt suited the low boat-shaped neckline. Her only make-up was her light foundation and a slick of eyeshadow. Her long pearl-quartz earrings completed the picture.

As the ancient clock on the landing chimed eight, she made her way downstairs. Oscar was standing at the bar, talking to Adam, and both men looked up as she approached, Oscar with a heightening of his pulse, which he tried to ignore.

As Helena approached, she smiled quickly, noting Oscar's undeniably sexy appearance. He was dressed in light trousers and designer jacket and open-neck shirt; his hair had been newly washed, the dark, determined jaw obviously clean-shaven. A perfect model for any advertisement, she thought instinctively.

Immediately, Adam came from behind the bar, two large menus in his hands, and beckoned the two to follow him, leading them over to a table in the far corner of the restaurant.

Holding Helena's chair out for her, he said, 'Tonight's special dish is seared sea bass—caught this morning,' he added proudly. Then he took the just-opened bottle of wine from the ice bucket on the table and filled their glasses. 'I'll be back for your order as soon as you've decided,' he said.

'He seems to run a very tight ship here,' Oscar commented, glancing at the man's retreating figure. 'By the way, I hope you approve of this...of my choice,' he said, picking up his glass.

How could Helena not approve? It was vintage champagne. She put the glass to her lips and sipped at the frothy bubbles, looking across at him steadily. 'Is this by way of a celebration?' she asked enigmatically.

Oscar raised a brow. 'If you like,' he said casually. Well, they had just been left a fortune. 'I hope you don't have a problem with champagne?'

Helena smiled briefly. 'I've only had it twice before—at weddings,' she said. 'And while I'm no connoisseur, I always found it a very...special...drink.' She paused. 'Thank you,' she added.

A muscle pounded in Oscar's jaw as he gazed across at her. She looked so unutterably lovely he couldn't keep his eyes off her. Her hair was shining, its thick bands glinting like gold in the flickering candlelight, but she did look pale, and he said briefly, 'Are you feeling OK now...has your headache really gone?'

'Absolutely,' Helena said lightly. 'And, as a matter of fact, I'm feeling quite hungry,' she added. She picked up her menu, hoping he didn't notice it trembling slightly between her fingers. In a thousand lifetimes could she ever have imagined she'd be so close to Oscar again? To breathe the same air that he was breathing? To watch that firm mouth with the immaculate teeth, white against his suntan? He wasn't merely good-looking, not merely handsome; he had that stunning, sultry, Mediterranean charisma that turned every gullible female heart to jelly.

As they gave Adam their order and waited for their meal to arrive, Oscar said, 'I've had time to think things over this afternoon and I can't help wondering if it's the right thing to be leaving the house unoccupied for so long.' He drank from his glass. 'There's a big problem with squatters taking over empty premises—certainly in London at the moment—and I understand that once they're in, it's difficult to get rid of them.' He frowned thoughtfully. 'Of course, I know that Benjamin and Louise will always be close at hand, but that wouldn't stop determined individuals from gaining entry on a dark night—and if that did happen it would certainly add to our problems.' He paused. 'Maybe we should consider a short-term let,' he added, 'as a safety measure.'

Helena could hardly believe what she'd just heard Oscar say. This could clinch it for her! Play right into her hands! Had her guardian angel—who'd been somewhat absent lately—decided to put in an appearance?

Presently, enjoying their meal—they'd both selected the sea bass with salad—Oscar said bluntly, 'So, perhaps we ought to catch up. What's been happening to you in the last ten years or so?' He speared a cherry tomato expertly with his fork. 'Isobel informed me that you got a place at a top London university.'

'Yes. Amazing, wasn't it?' Helena said lightly. 'Amazing that a modest secondary school in the sticks can take students to such elevated places.' She looked down quickly, hoping that hadn't sounded like a dig at his private boarding school education which had taken him to Cambridge, and later to Harvard.

She went on hurriedly. 'Anyway, I got a respectable degree in Economics and International Business Studies, and my present job is with the Harcourt Employment Agency,' she added, 'but, as I've mentioned, I hope to soon be on the move.'

'So, where next, then?' he enquired.

Without looking at him, Helena said, 'I'm not sure yet because I haven't made up my mind. I want to give myself time to really look around before deciding. And in the meantime, of course, temporary employment is not hard to find in the city.'

There was silence for a moment, then he said, 'You live alone?'

'Yes,' Helena replied promptly.

'So, no man in your life...no marriage ties on the horizon for you?'

Helena shook her head quickly. 'No.' She decided to lob the ball back to him. 'And you, Oscar? No wife and children at your beck and call?'

That familiar tilt of his upper lip. 'No,' he said flatly. 'I have a feeling that that's a rather unlikely scenario,' he added, before resuming his meal.

That remark didn't surprise Helena. He was obviously not the marrying kind, though there must be a permanent and very hopeful queue of women at his disposal. From his lofty perch in life he could look down, take his pick and walk away. Besides, mistresses were a far more convenient answer to the emotional needs of men like him, weren't they? No need to commit himself in any way.

He interrupted her thoughts. 'I can't help wondering why you're still free and single,' he said. 'London is a big city with plenty of men after beautiful women. How have you managed to escape their clutches?'

Helena felt a rush of pleasure at the remark—because it implied the sort of compliment she hadn't expected from Oscar. Not any more.

Then, feeling unusually relaxed, she went on, 'Not long after my father died, I did meet Jason, and we were together for some time.' She paused. 'He was a great help at the time and seemed to understand how I was feeling, how much I was missing not being able to ring my dad, tell him the latest news.' She sighed. 'When I look back, I realize Jason must have listened for hours to me feeling sorry for myself.' She looked across at Oscar quickly. 'Perhaps I should have grown up by then,' she added.

Oscar made no comment, but his eyes had softened at her words, realizing how much he was loving watching her mouth, the fleeting expressions on her face as she'd spoken. He'd always known that Helena's mother had died years ago, and that Daniel and his daughter had been extremely close, so it was natural that Daniel's death would have hit her hard. And, despite all outward appearances, he recognized that touching vulnerability about Helena that had always stirred him.

'Big cities can be very lonely places,' he said briefly.

Helena kept her eyes on her plate. She wasn't going to say anything at all about Mark, who she'd thought she'd been deeply in love with—and who she'd imagined had returned her feelings. Their unexpected break-up had hurt, and the split, when it happened, had come as a total shock. She didn't want to think about it ever again, or the fact that he'd cheated on her with an old mutual friend. But, even worse, Mark had told Helena that he found her cool and distant. He hadn't mentioned the word frigid, but the implication was there, and she was still finding it hard to accept.

'Anyway,' Helena went on, touching her lips with her napkin, 'eventually I realized that I was using Jason just as a shoulder to cry on, and that was hardly fair because I felt nothing for him, not really. He was nice, and very kind, but nothing more. It was time to let him go and stop wasting any more time on me.' She paused. 'And I still feel terribly guilty about it.'

She took a sip from her glass, then smiled briefly. 'But I needn't have worried about him. He soon found someone else, and I think they're engaged to be married.'

Oscar raised an eyebrow. 'Jason was obviously a man with a single-track purpose,' he said. And, after a moment, added, 'Each to his own, I suppose.'

Helena made no comment. Being a settled family man was never going to be on Oscar's agenda, she thought. How could she ever have thought otherwise?

As they were finishing the last of the meal, he said casually, 'My aunt was very upset about your father's death at the time... He'd been a valued member of her staff for so many years.' He paused. 'And he was still comparatively young, wasn't he?'

'He was fifty-nine,' Helena said shortly. 'I had already begun planning a party for his sixtieth birthday.'

There was quite a long silence after that, then Helena

said, in a deliberately bright tone, 'And your parents, Oscar? How are they?'

He paused before answering. 'My father no longer works…hasn't done for a long time. He and my mother live permanently in their place in Bermuda.' He reached across to refill their glasses. 'My uncle—my father's remaining brother—has also retired, so I am the only working family member left.'

The significance of what Oscar had just said didn't need to be spelt out. That he was the last in a long line and that, although it was unthinkable that the firm would ever founder, if he had no heirs the family name would inevitably die out.

'And of course Isobel was the last of her generation?' Helena asked.

'Yes, she was, and the only Englishwoman—the only "foreigner"—to infiltrate our community, our enclave,' Oscar replied. 'It had never been done before. But all the family loved her and, in spite of all the places she could have lived around the world, her base was always Mulberry Court. Though of course she travelled extensively when my uncle was alive.'

'Yes, I know,' Helena said. 'I was always fascinated by her description of all the places she'd seen. She made it all so real.'

By now, her third glass of champagne was having its effect on Helena—she seldom drank, and was unused to alcohol of this quality. She certainly hadn't expected to feel as comfortable as this with Oscar, not after all this time. Taking a grape from the cheese tray in front of them, she nibbled it thoughtfully and looked across at him.

'So, where do you live—usually, I mean?' she asked.

'Oh, here, there and everywhere,' he said casually. 'I've an apartment in London, a place in Greece and an apartment on the Upper East Side, New York, but I don't stay anywhere for long. I've never felt settled enough to put down any roots. I'm travelling so much all the time, but I suppose my place in Athens is my useful bolt-hole.'

Helena immediately remembered when he had promised to take her to his homeland one day, but she didn't voice her thoughts.

They'd finished their coffee and Helena picked up her almost full glass of champagne, drinking it down to the last drop. Then, after a few moments, she said slowly, her brow slightly furrowed in thought, 'You know, you may have a point about a possible squatter problem at Mulberry Court.' She paused. 'And I think I might have a solution to that, Oscar.'

'Oh?'

'Well…' She spoke carefully. 'I could arrange to come and stay at the house myself for a short while… Well, a month or so, at least.'

Oscar raised his eyebrows. 'Would that be possible?' he enquired. 'I mean—your present arrangements in London, your job…your current home?''

'Actually, it would fit in rather well,' Helena said casually. 'When I switch jobs—which I intend to do almost immediately—it'll mean I'm homeless because my cottage belongs to Simon Harcourt.' She hesitated. 'I feel I need a sort of breathing space in my life at the moment, and I'd certainly like to get out of London— even if it is just temporarily.'

Oscar pursed his lips, thinking about this for a second. 'The house is rather isolated, isn't it... Are you sure you like the idea of being there on your own?' he said.

Helena smiled briefly. 'I'm used to being on my own,' she said. 'Besides, the cottages are less than a minute's walk away...I'd always have Louise for company—and Benjamin is obviously always about as well.'

Oscar nodded slowly, feeling slightly surprised at Helena's suggestion, but agreeing that it would be a useful move for the moment. He shrugged.

'Well, why not?' he said. Mulberry Court belonged to Helena now, he thought—she had a perfect right to stay if she wanted to. 'When do you anticipate that this plan could be put into action?' he asked.

'By the beginning of May,' Helena said at once—there was no need to tell Oscar she'd already given in her notice. She looked up at him, her eyes shining at how easily her hopes had materialized. 'And I can always get temping work in Dorchester if I run short of funds.'

Oscar was about to offer some interim financial input—then thought better of it. Helena was an independent woman with clearly a very firm hold on her private affairs. And she'd already turned down one offer he'd made, in no uncertain terms.

'Just think—I shall be Mistress of Mulberry Court!' Helena said. 'It'll be like the games I used to play when I was a child...pretending, imagining things!' She knew she still felt totally overwhelmed at all that had happened in the last few days, and being here with Oscar was the most overwhelming thing of all! An excited giggle almost turned into an attack of hiccups as she pointlessly picked up her empty glass, then put it down again. And at once, seeing her flushed cheeks and re-alizing that Helena had no head for alcohol, Oscar got up and came round to her side of the table to help her to her feet.

'It's been a long day, and I think it's time you were in bed, Helena,' he said shortly.

Helena stood rather shakily and picked up her bag and, with Oscar's hand under her elbow, they made their way upstairs, pausing outside Helena's door for a second while she searched for her key. And with every masculine impulse urging him, Oscar was acutely aware of a treacherous warm tide of feeling in his groin. In any other circumstances, with any other woman, it would have been a foregone conclusion that he spent the night in her bed. With his hand lightly on the small of her back, he said, 'You're quite sure about all this—about staying by yourself at Mulberry Court?' He hesi-tated. 'If you change your mind, we can always get John Mayhew to find a suitable tenant.'

'There's absolutely no need for anyone else to live in our…in the house—not yet,' Helena said quickly, look-ing up at him, painfully conscious of his dark, magnetic gaze as he looked down at her in the subdued lighting. 'It's going to all work out *perfectly*,' she added. 'I just know it is.'

And in an insanely impulsive, grateful reflex action, she raised her head and kissed him lightly on the cheek before turning away, but not before Oscar's hand was at the back of her neck, pulling her around towards him firmly, pulling her face closer to his own.

But with every warning bell ringing in her head, Helena avoided his lips, her hands shaking so much that she dropped her key. She stooped quickly to pick it up, then unlocked her door and glanced back at him, smiling tremulously.

'Goodnight, Oscar,' she said.

Inside, Helena closed the door behind her and stood with her back against it for a few moments, waiting for her heart to stop almost leaping from her chest. She must have been *mad* to have kissed Oscar like that, she thought, because he'd obviously read something into it which she hadn't meant! She'd only given him a brief peck on the cheek, that was all! A sort of normal thing to someone she'd known for such a long time...

But with her skin tingling at the thought, Helena knew that Oscar had wanted to kiss her! She kept repeating the thought over and over in her mind... He'd wanted to kiss her and somehow, *somehow*, she'd managed to turn away! She'd managed to avoid the very dream she had so often relived in her mind. How had she managed to stop herself from collapsing into those strong arms, feeling the weight of him against her, letting that manly, musky smell of him ignite all her primitive instincts...?

But she *had* managed it. Because she'd been there before, she reminded herself bleakly—and she was never going to risk another unhappy ending like the one which had driven her to unimaginable despair.

* * *

In his own room two doors away, Oscar stood by the window for a few moments, clenching his jaw. He'd just had the unique experience of being turned down by a woman!

The sensuous mouth twisted as he let his mind dwell on the what-might-have-been... He would now be slowly undressing her, he thought, caressing her, using all his natural abilities to inflame her, to make her want him as much as he had wanted her.

He turned away abruptly. In the bathroom, he had a cold shower then dried himself briskly, drawing the huge towel back and forth across his tanned shoulders, his glistening muscles flexing and hardening with the effort. Catching a sight of himself in the mirror, he leaned forward thoughtfully. His brow seemed to be developing more lines every time he looked, he thought.

As for Helena...Helena was still as dove-soft, as flawless, as she had been on the first day he'd set eyes on her.

CHAPTER FOUR

HELENA woke the following morning having had the most blissful night's sleep she could ever remember. A night full of dreams in which she'd lain in Oscar's arms, felt his lips claim hers over and over again, felt his hands trace the curves of her body...the sort of dreams which she had stopped having a very long time ago. But last night it had been so wonderful, so real, she had awoken, her heart drumming wildly, and had fully expected to see him there, raised above her, his eyes alight with desire...

Now, she sat up and rested her head on her knees. It was so stupid of her to have given him that peck on the cheek, she told herself again. And what hot-blooded, alpha male—especially one like Oscar Theotokis— ever resisted an opportunity? Yet Helena was honest enough to admit that another millisecond, and she would have been helpless in his arms. Because, in spite of everything, she knew she probably still loved Oscar, was still in love with him, even after all these years. And the pathetic position she was in was dangerous, because he didn't love her, not any more, and he probably never had. Lust and love were two entirely different things—everyone knew that—and it was lust undoubtedly fuelled by that amazing champagne that he must have been feeling last night. Even so, she acknowledged a shiver of pleasure at the thought.

She got out of bed and went into the bathroom, groaning at the sight of herself. Her hair was all over the place and needed immediate attention if she was to face Oscar with no telltale signs of the restless night they had shared—if only in her dreams! She'd be sitting opposite him in an hour, having breakfast and making desultory conversation—and hoping that nothing in her eyes or manner would reveal the emotion still simmering just below the surface of her thoughts.

With rugged determination, Helena forced herself to concentrate on the present. One good thing was, she'd be able to tell Simon tomorrow that she was definitely leaving his employment. She made a face as she recalled her boss's persistent, unwanted attentions. No, she wouldn't be sorry to leave the Harcourt Agency, she thought. Though she would miss the other girls, plus the salary, she had to admit.

It was funny, she thought, as she smoothed lotion over her arms and body, that although she'd come to accept that she'd been left a considerable inheritance, she just couldn't take it in, or what it might eventually mean to her when the house was sold. She certainly did not want any money in the meantime, as Oscar had suggested, because until the sale of the house, there really wasn't any. Not really. It was still all on paper.

The far more important reason for her to feel almost dizzy with excitement was that Oscar had seemed quite happy for her to stay at Mulberry Court for a while. It would have been *so* embarrassing if he'd found a reason to object. But he hadn't.

Suddenly, a wave of optimism ran through Helena. She had just taken a very big step to tread a new path. And somehow she felt it was the right thing to do at this particular point. And now she had the prospect of spending spring and early summer in the place she loved best in all the world. Could it get any better?

She got ready and presently went downstairs to the restaurant. Oscar was already there, and when he saw her approach he stood up without smiling, and Helena coloured slightly. Did he remember their brief encounter last night? His undeniable gesture of familiarity? If he did, his expression gave nothing away. He was wearing casual trousers and a jacket, his round-neck, fine grey T-shirt exhibiting taut, well-toned muscles, and she deliberately avoided looking at him.

'Hello... Did you sleep well?' he said slowly, his voice seductively smooth, even at this early hour. Helena sat down on the chair he'd pulled out for her, tucking a stray frond of hair behind her ear.

'Very well, thank you,' she said, surprised at how easy it was to tell a blatant lie. She picked up the breakfast menu even though she didn't feel like much to eat. 'You?' she enquired.

'I seldom sleep more than four, maybe five hours,' he said. 'So I've been able to get some work done.' He shrugged briefly. 'As a matter of fact it looks as if I have to go back to Athens tomorrow. I'd hoped to be in the UK until the end of April... So if there's anything at all that we can sort out today, that would help,' he added, omitting to make the point that they could have done quite a lot if Helena had fallen in with his wish to more or less empty the house of its contents straight away.

He raised a hand to summon the waiter to take their breakfast order. 'We can at least talk with Benjamin about the grounds,' he went on, 'because it's obvious that he needs to be retained until further notice, and it would have been good to have seen Louise, too... Whatever happens, the property must be adequately maintained for the next twelve months.'

Helena adjusted the knife beside her plate carefully and picked up her napkin. It was obviously back to business this morning, she thought. That spontaneous, fleetingly amorous gesture of Oscar's last night hadn't meant anything at all—and he'd obviously completely forgotten about it. Well, that was no surprise—and that was good—wasn't it?

Later, as Oscar drove smoothly out of the car park, Helena settled herself back into the luxurious passenger seat and stared out of the window. So far, not a single mention had been made of her wish to stay at Mulberry Court. She hoped that he wasn't regretting it—or maybe he'd forgotten about that too, she thought.

But, as if reading her thoughts, he said, without looking at her, 'So, there are obviously going to be quite a few details of your own to sort out, Helena... What are you going to do about your personal belongings, your furniture?'

'Oh, I don't have very much at all,' Helena assured him quickly. 'I've only ever lived in furnished accommodation,' she explained, 'and before the cottage I shared with Anna, my friend from university. But she got married last year.'

Helena paused before going on. 'So, apart from books—rather a lot of books, I must admit—and clothes and bedding—and a few pictures, of course,' she went on, 'that's about it. It's only a few things so I'll be travelling very light,' she added.

Oscar smiled inwardly. He could already picture the sight of Helena's elderly car crammed to the roof with her 'few things'. And judging by everything he'd seen her wearing so far—including today's choice of a soft jade cashmere knit over skinny jeans—the contents of her wardrobe would probably take up most of the space.

They eventually came to the narrow road which led to Mulberry Court, and almost at once the cottages came into view and Helena leaned forward excitedly.

'Oh, look—Louise is there in the garden!' she exclaimed.

'She must have got back yesterday afternoon,' Oscar said, 'and there's Benjamin coming down the path—with Rosie, his adored hound,' he added.

Helena felt a surge of happiness at seeing the black Retriever bounding around the gardener's feet. The cottage wouldn't be the same without a dog, she thought. The fact that Bella, their black Labrador, had had to be put down just a couple of weeks before Daniel had died so suddenly had only added to Helena's sense of loss at the time. It was as if her father and the dog had refused to be separated.

Oscar drew the car to a halt, and he and Helena got out. At once Louise turned in surprise, then ran up and threw her arms around Helena's neck, hugging her tightly.

'Well, what a *wonderful* surprise to see you—and you, Mr Oscar,' she added, smiling up diffidently.

'I didn't expect that we'd see you this weekend, Louise,' Oscar began, and Louise cut in.

'No, well, I wasn't going to come back until Tuesday, but I don't like the house to be unattended for too long, and anyway I was beginning to feel homesick—isn't that silly?' Louise's open, friendly face broke into another grin and Helena thought—no, that's not silly. That's not silly at all.

By this time Rosie was determined to be noticed, winding her body around and around Helena's legs and barking, and Helena immediately bent to make a fuss of the dog.

'What a lovely animal,' she said, trying to avoid a very wet kiss on the nose.

Oscar spoke again. 'Helena, let me introduce you. Benjamin—this is Helena… Her father was my aunt's right-hand man for many years, doing the job you're doing. Before Helena went away to university she lived here in the cottage, so there isn't anything she doesn't know about Mulberry Court and its surroundings.'

Benjamin, a tall man, with a mass of unruly greying hair, shook Helena's hand warmly. 'Louise has told me all about your father, Helena, and I can only hope to keep up the standards he set here.'

Helena flushed with pride. 'We were walking in the grounds yesterday, Benjamin, and everything looked wonderful,' she assured him.

Louise pulled Helena towards her again. 'What are

we standing out here for?' she demanded. 'Come in, and let me make us all some coffee.'

'Thanks, but I must be getting on,' Benjamin said, clicking his fingers for the dog to follow him, and after they'd made their farewells the others went into Louise's warm and cosy cottage.

Presently, as they sat drinking their coffee, Oscar said, 'Have you been informed of the terms of my great-aunt's will, Louise?'

Louise looked away, her expression troubled. 'Only that I'm to receive a very generous sum of money,' she said. 'And also that I've been asked to stay on here until the…um…future of the house is decided.' She sighed. 'It will be so terrible to think of new owners taking over,' she added. 'But I know it's got to happen, and everyone has to face unpleasant changes from time to time.'

'Well, you needn't worry about that yet,' Oscar said. He paused, clearing his throat. 'Actually, my aunt has left the entire estate jointly between Helena and myself, but there is to be no sale for a year. And…' he shot a quick glance at Helena '…as a matter of fact, in a few weeks' time Helena will be coming to live at Mulberry Court herself.'

Louise's face lit up with delight. 'Well, I shall sleep easy for the first time since Mrs Theotokis died,' she said firmly. 'I hate not knowing what's going on—and Benjamin has been worried, too. We'd imagined we'd be packing our bags by now.'

Oscar put his cup down and stood up. 'Although we were up at the house yesterday, we need to take another look around today,' he said, looking down at Louise. 'Something might occur to us that could be done now.'

'I've been up there most days since Isobel died,' Louise said. 'Opened all the windows and kept the dust down.'

'Yes, we thought everything looked as perfect as ever, Louise—' Helena broke in '—including the lovely flower arrangement on the dining room table.'

Louise nodded. 'You'll have noticed that I've kept the Aga going—well, Benjamin and I take it in turns,' she added. Then, 'I emptied the fridge but not the freezer—and I haven't gone through the kitchen cupboards, either.' She hesitated. 'I didn't really know how much I should do for the time being. Mulberry Court has felt rather like a ship without a captain,' she added.

'Well, we'll be more of a crew now, Louise,' Helena said, 'as soon as I've settled things up in London. I should be back in three, four weeks at the most.'

Oscar and Helena left the cottage and after a second Louise followed them. 'Here—you'll want to make yourselves a drink up there,' she said, handing Helena a pint of milk. 'And if there's anything you need, just shout.'

As they drove slowly up the drive towards the house, Helena glanced across at Oscar. 'Isobel was lucky to have such a loyal person working for her all that time, wasn't she?'

Oscar tilted his head to one side. 'My aunt obviously appreciated her very much.' He narrowed his eyes briefly, thinking that it was good that Louise would be staying on at the cottage because it would be company for Helena while she was staying here.

He drew the car smoothly to a halt, and they both got out and started walking towards the main entrance of the house. The weather was bright with a high wind, making Helena's loosely tied hair fly wildly, almost covering her face for a second or two. As they got to the large oak front door, she tucked her hair safely behind her ears and reached into her bag for the keys to the house.

'My turn to open up today,' she said lightly, glancing up.

Inside, every corner of the place was lit up by shafts of strong morning sunlight and, as Oscar followed Helena into the kitchen, he said, 'I'll go and find Benjamin, tell him he'll be needed here for the next twelve months.' He paused. 'Of course, the new owners may decide to keep him on when the time comes. Left unattended, the place would be a wilderness in no time,' he added.

Helena didn't need reminding of that. It had always been a full-time job for her father, who'd only ever hired extra help in the autumn for harvesting the fruit.

She put her bag and the bottle of milk down and glanced up at Oscar. 'I liked him—Benjamin,' she said. 'He seemed really nice, and he and Louise seemed happy enough, relaxed enough, together, didn't they? It could have been really difficult if they hadn't got on—living next door to each other.' She smiled. 'And that lovely dog...Benjamin obviously worships her,' she added.

Oscar nodded. 'Yes, his luck really changed when my aunt interviewed him.'

Helena looked up curiously. 'Oh?'

'Apparently he had lost his job in the city and was staying with a friend in the area who told him about the vacancy at Mulberry Court. When Isobel heard his story she considered that Benjamin's genuine longing to be out in the open air—and his determination to learn quickly and to work hard if she'd give him the opportunity—were sufficient reasons to employ him.'

'What caused all the problems?' Helena asked.

'Oh, it was a common scenario…successful city trader is unexpectedly made redundant, loses his wife and his home all at the same time…' Oscar said. 'There are apparently two children involved as well, who he doesn't get to see very often. So Isobel decided that Mulberry Court might be just the thing for him to turn his life around. And from all outward appearances, she seems to have been right,' he added.

Oscar turned and went towards the door. 'I shan't be long,' he said, not looking back.

After he'd gone, Helena stood looking around her and marvelled again that this all now belonged to *her*… well, almost…and not just the house, but everything in it! And although it was to be only for one year, she was going to make the most of every second of the time she'd be staying here. And finding her way around the kitchen again would be a good start.

As Louise had said, the fridge was empty and had been turned off, but the freezer was still reasonably full of the usual staple items, none of which had yet exceeded their sell-by date, Helena noted, as she searched through the contents. This would still be OK for her own use when she returned in what she hoped would only be a couple of weeks.

The numerous cupboards held everything she'd need to keep herself fed while she was living here, and she could always shop for more, she thought, as she looked along the shelves. All the basic ingredients necessary for simple cooking were there, neatly arranged in Louise's usual way. Helena smiled briefly. She was looking forward to having some time to cook for herself here in this wonderful kitchen, where all that time ago Isobel's housekeeper had shown her most of the tricks of the trade.

After a while, she left the kitchen and wandered again through the rooms on the ground floor, before going slowly up the wide staircase. She paused for a moment to gaze out of the long landing windows at the garden beyond, biting her lip. It was really difficult to think of this place as belonging to her, she thought, whatever it said in Isobel's will. This was a Theotokis property—Oscar was a Theotokis so it was obviously different for him. But she was the outsider. And once the house was sold next year, there would never be a reason for her to come near the place ever again.

Back down in the kitchen, Helena glanced up at the big clock on the wall. It was almost lunch time, and Oscar still hadn't come back. She suddenly remembered the food she'd seen in the freezer and there were several packets of unopened staples in the cupboard, and they could have tea or coffee with the milk Louise had given them. Enough for a simple meal, Helena thought, setting the things out on the table. She wondered, idly, when he intended going back to London…

He obviously wouldn't be leaving it late because he'd said he would be flying back to Greece tomorrow, and anyway, she herself needed to leave in an hour or so. She wanted to be in the office early tomorrow, to start clearing her desk and tying up ends.

She decided to make some tea—she was certainly ready for some, she realized. She put out two mugs and plates and knives, then went over to fill the kettle, her mind going over and over all her hopes and plans and trying to keep her developing feelings for Oscar firmly out of her thoughts.

She stood waiting for a couple of minutes until the kettle came to boiling point, then she picked it up and was just starting to pour when Oscar returned, a sudden gust making the back door slam behind him loudly, and Helena automatically jumped, turning quickly, before letting out a shriek of pain as a stream of boiling water coursed over her hand and arm, almost making her drop the kettle on the floor. 'Ow... Oh... Ow!' she cried desperately. *'Ow!'*

Immediately seeing what had happened, Oscar cursed out loud.

'Heleena!' he exclaimed, reaching her in three long strides, and taking the kettle from her. Then, turning the cold tap on full, he grasped her hand and held it under the gushing water while Helena winced in agony.

For several minutes they both just stood there, Oscar not letting go of Helena's hand from under the running water, looking down at her, his eyes intense with concern as Helena tried hard to take control of herself.

'That was the most idiotic thing I've done in a long time,' she wailed, almost crying with the unbelievable pain. She automatically leaned into Oscar, who had put his arm tightly around her waist to support her, and presently the anguish began to lessen and he gently let her go, passing her some tissues from the box on the counter top. He bent his head to examine her reddening flesh, muttering incomprehensible oaths under his breath.

'Oh...*agapi mou*,' he said softly, and Helena closed her eyes at the memory of that expression of endearment she hadn't heard for so long, and even after all this time it sent a tremor of warmth through her thighs right down to her toes.

After a few moments, seeing how shocked it had made her, he led Helena over to the table to sit down, glancing at the few things she'd laid out for their lunch. 'You really shouldn't have gone to all this trouble,' he joked.

She dabbed her hand very cautiously with the tissues, not looking at him. Her skin wasn't broken, she noted gratefully. But it was bright red and the incident had given her a horrible fright, making her tremble visibly. And Oscar had seen it.

Without saying any more, he went over to make the tea, before bringing it across to Helena. 'Here,' he said gently, 'drink this—it'll help.'

After a few cautious sips, Helena pulled herself together and glanced up at him. 'So...you obviously saw Benjamin,' she said, trying to act normally, and Oscar nodded.

'Yes, he was more than happy to be here for another year. At least he's being given time to come to terms with the prospect of yet another dramatic change in his personal circumstances.'

As she tried to nibble at a biscuit, Helena said, 'And we know that he and Louise will take good care of Mulberry Court for the time being,' she added.

Oscar took a mouthful of some of the food Helena had prepared before speaking. 'Have you seen anything in the house that you might want to take away with you, I mean eventually, apart from the figures?' he asked, and Helena cut in.

'No, nothing. Anyway, I shall have more time to consider it when I come back,' she said. 'I intend returning to London early this afternoon…after I've picked up my things and paid my bill at the Inn,' she added.

'I've already settled our bill there,' Oscar said casually, and Helena looked at him quickly. She hadn't realized he'd already paid for their stay.

'How much do I owe you?' she asked, reaching for her bag.

Oscar paused. 'I've forgotten,' he said, taking another biscuit from the plate. 'but I remember thinking it was very reasonable.'

Helena opened her purse. 'Well, then, try and remember,' she said firmly. He needn't act Mr Philanthropist, she thought, just because he was unbelievably rich. She had more than enough money to pay her own way.

'Forget it,' he said. 'It's not important.'

Helena sighed, but decided to let the matter drop. She wasn't in the mood for any arguments—and anyway, she'd never win one with Oscar. She sipped at her tea again, aware that they were now sitting so close their knees and thighs were touching under the table. She knew she could have moved away slightly, but she didn't want to. The warmth of him was comforting... more than comforting...and she had to choke back the sensuous thoughts that would come bubbling up every time she was anywhere near him. Fate had been kind— and cruel—at the same time, she decided. She had been left an inheritance she could never have dreamed of, but it meant that the drop dead gorgeous Greek who'd long ago stolen her heart was here with her again, temporarily part of her life. And she didn't need it, because he didn't want her—or any woman. Helena swallowed at the depth of her own feelings. She had to face facts. Whatever their present circumstances, there was never going to be a future for her and Oscar, so she must try and deal with the here and now sensibly... *Sensibly?*... What part did sense play where matters of the heart were concerned?

Realizing that they hadn't spoken for several moments, he took her hand and said softly, 'Is it still hurting very much, *Heleena?*' And as she looked up at him Helena wanted to say, *Oh, yes, it still hurts... You'll never know how much, Oscar...* But instead she attempted a cool reply.

'No...no—I can hardly feel anything at all now,' she said, wiping a stray tear from her cheek. 'Just a very slight burning sensation, that's all.' And admitting the double meaning in those words made Helena's blue eyes limpid with hopelessness.

Then, as his unflinching gaze enslaved her once more, Oscar slowly raised her hand and pressed it gently to his lips. 'There,' he said huskily, looking down at her, 'let me make it feel better...'

In the next few moments of suspended silence, broken only by the gentle ticking of the clock, nothing could have prepared Helena for what was about to happen, because, with time standing still, Oscar slowly got to his feet, scraping back his chair, and pulled her up towards him, closing his mouth over her parted lips with expert precision. She gasped, the unexpectedness of what was happening taking her completely by surprise, and something vital, electrical, leapt from her at the urgency of his kiss...leaving her breathless.

'Oscar...' she faltered—this was not happening! Not again! She must not let it! She couldn't bear it!

But it was too late. Much too late. She was in his arms, surrendering to his lithe, powerful physique, helpless and ecstatic. Then, frightened at what was happening to her, she managed to pull away slightly and look up at him, at his dark eyes, aflame with desire, boring into hers...

'Oscar...this is not...I must leave...' Helena began, but as she tried to protest he took advantage of her open mouth to claim it again and again, his kisses deep, penetrating, leaving her breathless with longing.

'Heleena...kardia mou.' The dark passion in his voice sounded like the guttural growl of an animal about to claim its prey, and Helena pulled away properly, stepping back, her eyes full of fear.

'It's too late, Oscar,' she whispered. 'For us it's much, much too late.'

* * *

An hour later, they drove back to the Inn to collect their belongings, Helena sitting silently, choking back tears.

As Oscar had kissed her so thoroughly she had been in paradise—a paradise once lost, and so briefly regained. But wait a minute, she was not the inexperienced female she had once been, she told herself again—this was *now*! And there was no going back. That kiss had been a gesture—a gesture born of fleeting male sympathy—but then, being Oscar, it had very quickly become something much more. More vital, more intense, and yes, more thrilling. It would be wrong to deny it, wrong to pretend that she hadn't wanted it to go on and on. She had not known another man who could match his sensitive, sensual, unforgettable technique.

She cast a fleeting glance at him, at the stern profile, the determined chin, and her shoulders drooped. For him, she thought, it would have been merely a case of déjà vu, something to be enjoyed for old times' sake...

Today had been a bad mistake, a terrible mistake, she thought, and now she couldn't wait to be by herself. Away from temptation, away from him.

And Oscar, keeping his concentration on the road ahead, had arrived at one of his usual, unequivocal decisions. Time was precious, and limited. Time was finite, and life was short and he didn't intend to waste any more of it. Using every ounce of ingenuity, he would have to make her understand. And trust him. But love him?

Oscar allowed himself an inward smile. Oh, yes, he knew he could make her love him again. The memory of the way she had responded to his ardour proved that Helena was still the warm, passionate female she'd always been. And would be again...with him.

CHAPTER FIVE

THREE weeks later, very early in the morning, Oscar took a brief glance around his large air-conditioned office high above the bustling streets of Athens, before packing his essential belongings into the large business holdall that went everywhere with him. His secretary had arranged for a car to be outside to take him to the airport where his private jet would be waiting, and now he walked swiftly towards the lift. He knew he would have to return again on Monday, but now there were other things than business on his mind. Or, rather, another person on his mind. And he knew that today she was returning to Dorset.

As the jet flew him rapidly across the ice-blue skies towards Heathrow Airport, Oscar gazed thoughtfully out of the window. Since meeting Helena again, it seemed to him that the planet had tilted somewhat on its axis, throwing things into slight confusion. He leaned back in the luxurious chair, stretching out his legs in front of him. Whatever else was happening to the world, the one thing he was certain of was that he needed to be with Helena... Being away from her was solving nothing, and he'd been away for far too long. Ten years too long.

* * *

It was turning out to be a very warm day, and Helena pushed up the sleeves of her top and went on vacuuming the carpets, before taking a final look around the cottage to make sure everything was clean and tidy, and to check that she was not leaving anything behind.

Her last weeks in the office had gone better than she could have hoped because Simon had hardly been there at all, and all the other girls had been happy for her—if rather envious at her news. They'd had a very jolly farewell lunch together, with Helena giving them the address she'd be staying at—and them threatening to visit her en masse—and as she'd waved them a last goodbye, she had to admit to a mixture of feelings. From the safety of normality and routine, she was about to tread an unknown path…and she fervently hoped she was doing the right thing.

But filling her mind and overriding every other thought was the way that Oscar had kissed her that afternoon. She'd tried to stop thinking about it ever since, tried to convince herself that it hadn't meant anything to him. But did she want it to mean anything? Was she kidding herself that any relationship that might fleetingly blossom between them now, under these particular and very unusual circumstances, would end any differently than the last time? Helena sighed. She knew the answer to that. She knew she must force herself to be realistic.

She stopped what she was doing for a moment, wiping her forehead with the back of her hand, remembering how, later, after picking up their belongings from the Inn, they hadn't said much, making a very casual departure in their separate cars, with Oscar merely saying a brief, 'Take care,' to her through her open window. And she'd only heard from him once since— a rather hurried phone call, obviously from his office because she'd heard men's loud voices raised in the background. It was a rather blunt request that he be 'informed' when she expected to take up residency at Mulberry Court. She shrugged as she thought about that. Well, he did have a vested interest in the place, she thought, and was clearly anxious for it not to be unoccupied for too long. So, by going to live there temporarily, she was doing them both a favour, she told herself firmly.

Now, she picked up her duvet and went outside to put it in the back of the car, which by now was crammed to the roof. She hadn't realized just how much she'd accumulated since she'd been living here, but at least her bedding would help to keep everything safe, she thought, as she tucked it firmly around her belongings. Her cases and bags of clothes were in the boot, and she'd wrapped towels around her few pieces of china and glassware, but she'd had to use the passenger seat and the floor-well for most of her books and CDs. It had been something of a major exercise to pack everything, she admitted, pushing back a tendril of hair from her flushed forehead.

She locked up for the last time, determined to go without a backward glance. She *had* been happy living here, she thought, but that part of her life was in the past and she had somewhere else to go now—just for a bit—and London would still be here waiting for her when she returned.

With her heart doing somersaults of excitement—

and a little apprehension—she switched on the car's engine, her eyes widening in concern at the response. Instead of roaring into life—which, despite its age, it usually did—there was only a sort of wheeze, a cough…and nothing! Oh, *no!* The car had been so good-tempered of late. *Please, not today of all days*, she implored it. She waited a few seconds before trying again—she'd once been told that was what you should do—but the result was almost the same, except this time it didn't even cough, and the wheeze was only a gentle breathy whisper of protest.

Since her experience of car maintenance was nil, Helena knew that she had one option—she'd have to call the road service people and hope that someone could arrive soon because, apart from wanting to get going on her journey, the inside of the car was becoming like an oven.

She took her mobile from her bag and, after a few abortive tries, she got through to someone who told her that, unfortunately, it was unlikely anyone could arrive for about two hours. The fact that she was not stranded on an isolated road and was actually outside her own front door seemed to weigh against her, Helena thought, as she gave an exasperated sigh. She rang off, biting her lip, annoyed that she hadn't bothered to get the car serviced; she knew she should have done it by now, but it was usually so reliable and it was one of the things she'd let slip. Well, there'd been a lot on her mind lately, she excused herself, resting her head back against the seat.

Suddenly her mobile rang and she jumped, her spirits rising. Perhaps someone could come now after all.

It was Oscar! And although just to hear his voice sent her heart soaring, Helena made a face to herself. She'd have to tell him her present position, and for some reason she didn't want to, didn't want to sound pathetic. She should have been on her way by now.

'Helena—have you arrived?' The deep voice sent Helena's nerves all over the place, as usual.

She swallowed. 'Oh…hello…no, not yet,' she said, clearing her throat. 'My car refuses to start, and no one can come to sort me out for a couple of hours so I'll just have to sit it out until…'

'Where are you?' Oscar cut in abruptly.

Helena gritted her teeth. She'd have to own up. 'I'm outside my front door—my ex-front door,' she said. 'I haven't been able to move as much as a yard up the road. I'm sitting here surrounded by all my stuff… In fact, there's only just room for me,' she added, keeping her voice deliberately light. She didn't want to make a fuss—and anyway, she was sure to get to Mulberry Court by nightfall.

There was barely a moment's pause before he said breezily, 'Oh, well, that's life.' And with that he ended the call, and Helena smiled briefly. He really was determined to make sure he knew what was going on, she thought, but it was really good to hear from him, she admitted.

Presently, she glanced at her watch. It was gone two and, feeling thirsty, she reached for the bottle of water she'd packed and took a long drink. Surely someone should be here soon, she thought, sitting back and closing her eyes.

Even with all the windows open it was hot and sultry in the car with not even a breath of air to relieve the humidity. After a few minutes, despite all her efforts to stay awake, Helena's eyelids began to droop. Once or twice she made herself sit up straighter, before relapsing again into a state of torpor, until at last she couldn't stop herself from drifting off, her semi-consciousness full of thoughts tumbling in on more thoughts and through it all the sound of Oscar's voice, gentle but insistent. Her lips tilted in a smile as she heard him apologizing, over and over again, for disturbing her.

Then, more strongly, 'It does seem a shame to disturb you, *Heleena*,' the voice repeated, 'but we have places to go, things to do...'

Suddenly, Helena woke up properly and with a gasp of amazement she found herself looking up into Oscar's amused eyes. Several seconds passed before she gained possession of her senses and was able to speak.

'Oscar... What on earth? I mean...why are you? What are you doing here? Why aren't you in Greece?' she stuttered foolishly.

'Because I'm here to make sure you get safely to Mulberry Court...today, if possible,' he added wryly.

Helena gazed up at him unbelievingly. If you thought someone was hundreds of miles away and suddenly he appeared in front of you like an apparition, it was distinctly unnerving, she excused herself.

'I flew in early today,' he said. 'I needed to see someone in the London office and thought I'd check up on you, see if you were OK,' he added casually.

Helena got out of the car, then saw the four-by-four parked alongside and, before she could say anything,

Oscar said, 'I knew we'd never get all your belongings in the Ferrari so I hired this instead.' He peered into Helena's car. 'And I think I did the right thing,' he added bluntly.

Helena looked at him, slightly mystified. 'But...what are we going to do about my car?' she said. 'We just can't leave it here—and what about the person who's supposed to be coming?'

'Ring the company again now,' Oscar instructed her. 'Tell them you've left the keys at your local dealers—they're only half a mile away from here—and then they can either drive it or tow it there. We'll arrange for the garage to keep the car there until further notice and pick it up at some point in the future.' He glanced at his watch. 'In the meantime, I'll start loading up.'

Feeling extremely thankful—though rather dazed—at the formidable way Oscar was taking over, Helena rang the road organization again, who seemed more than ready to do as she asked, especially as it meant that now there was less urgency for them to send out a mechanic.

She snapped her mobile shut, then began passing things to Oscar as he deftly fitted everything neatly into the four-by-four. As she started heaving one of the heavy boxes of books from the passenger seat of her car, he came up quickly behind her, taking it from her.

'I remember you saying you had rather a lot of books,' he said, smiling down at her briefly.

Helena took a deep breath, intensely conscious of him standing so close to her. He was wearing designer jeans and a cream rugby shirt, and his hair, shining black and glossy, had fallen forward onto his forehead, making him look boyish and carefree—just as she remembered him…

Later, with everything safely stowed in the larger vehicle, Oscar began driving slowly away from the area. He glanced across at her. 'Did you have a fairly smooth exit from the job?' he enquired briefly.

'Yes, there was no problem,' Helena replied, remembering Simon's very formal last few words to her in front of everyone. Still, that was all in the past, she thought, her spirits lifting at the thought of the immediate future and what lay ahead.

'I don't suppose you've been able to have anything to eat yet, have you? It's well past lunch time… Would you like to stop somewhere?'

Helena glanced at him quickly. 'What about you?'

He shrugged. 'I had quite a serious meal on the flight,' he began, and Helena interrupted.

'I'm not a great fan of on-board food,' she said. 'What did they give you?'

Oscar half smiled. 'They gave me what I ordered,' he said briefly and, without looking at her, 'I was using the company jet,' he added.

Helena looked out of her window, annoyed at her stupidity. Of course. Did she imagine that Oscar Theotokis would have been mixing with the rest of humanity on a routine morning flight? Even if it would have been first class? No, he'd arrived on his very own aircraft. She sighed, her hands clasped tightly in her lap. It must be weird, she thought, to have access to such incredible wealth, to give any instruction, any order, and know that money would buy it.

'So, shall we stop for something to eat?' he asked.

'No, I'd rather go on,' Helena said quickly. 'And, anyway, I did pack a picnic. Maybe we can stop and have it later.'

They drove in silence for a while, each with their own thoughts, Oscar headily aware of how beautiful Helena was looking, dressed in a pair of white jeans and a golden yellow top, her hair tied back in one long ponytail. She always appeared so effortlessly chic, he thought, licking his top lip briefly.

Three long weeks had passed since he'd held her in his arms, since he'd felt her soft lips mould with his. Despite everything else going on, she had never left his thoughts…his desperate thoughts of wanting her. So how much longer was it going to be…? How much longer was he prepared to wait? But strategy was everything, he reminded himself, and if he moved in too quickly he might lose her again, and this time it would be for good.

Helena, her head resting back against the seat, wondered if Oscar had given so much as a single thought to the way he'd practically overpowered her, both physically and emotionally, that afternoon in the kitchen. His momentary passion had been hot, fiery, ruthlessly demanding yet exquisitely tender all at the same time. The sort of sensations that had been missing from her life for so very, very long. The sort of sensations she'd never expected to feel again. But did he remember how fired up they had both been? And if he did, had it mattered to him since? Today, his attitude had been friendly, businesslike in sorting out her problems for her, but he wasn't here because of her. He was only in

England because of a business necessity. It was a total fluke that she was sitting here with him now.

The May weather couldn't have been more wonderful as they drove swiftly towards their destination. They'd left the motorway a long time ago, and were now making their way through a much prettier region. Sitting on the high seat of the large vehicle, Helena was able to look right out and view the countryside as it rolled past them, most of the trees in full leaf. And every now and then she could see a hilly field dotted with sheep and dozens of tiny lambs. She took a deep breath. This sort of environment just had to be better than the stuffy streets of the city, she thought. She was going to make the most of the next couple of months, she told herself.

Presently Oscar said, 'Would you like to stop for your picnic now? There seem to be suitable places I can pull in.'

Helena suddenly realized how hungry she was feeling. 'Yes—thanks,' she said briefly, cringing inwardly as she thought about her 'picnic'. All she'd done was to empty the fridge of its remaining contents—which were one tomato, a small piece of cucumber, a lemon, a rather sad-looking mushroom and a roll. Plus a chocolate biscuit. Hardly an exciting meal, and not much of it, she thought, because she'd have to ask Oscar to share it. But she had made a good flask of coffee, which she hoped was still reasonably hot. She wondered, rather enviously, what he'd had to eat on the plane…obviously a world away from the rather pathetic things in her holdall.

Within a few minutes Oscar pulled into a lay-by

next to a farm gate, and they both got out of the vehicle, Oscar raising his arms above his head and stretching.

'It is beautiful around here,' he commented, glancing across at Helena, who had already opened the gate and spotted a suitable place just inside to set out the food. She was kneeling down and taking things from her bag and she looked up at him as he joined her.

'When I said "picnic" I think I was exaggerating,' she said lightly. 'This is all the food there was left in the fridge. I hope you weren't expecting anything exceptional.'

'I wasn't expecting anything,' he said, 'because I've already eaten. So it's all for you.'

'Well, I can guarantee the coffee,' Helena said, 'but we'll have to share.' She shot him a rather diffident glance, aware of the easy familiarity of what she'd just said. The words had just slipped off her tongue, and she was rewarded with one of Oscar's dark, lazy half-smiles as he looked down at her.

Helena uncorked the flask and carefully poured some coffee into the plastic top, before handing it to him. And, as their eyes met, an unspoken thought passed between them. Helena forced her gaze away from him. For herself, she couldn't even begin to express her own feelings at this precise moment, only that in these surroundings she felt safe, secure—and almost deliriously happy—to be here with Oscar. A month ago, this present scenario would have been unthinkable. If only she could stop the clock now, she thought…to fix time.

Not feeling at all bothered that she was eating and Oscar wasn't, Helena bit into the tomato carefully, before breaking off a piece of the roll and putting it into her mouth. And, after a moment, he sat down beside her to drink the coffee.

It didn't take long for Helena to eat what she wanted and soon, replacing what was left into her bag, she looked around her, shading her eyes with her hand. 'Oh, look! I can hardly believe it!' she said. 'There are cowslips in this field. I haven't seen any of those for so long!'

'Cowslips?' Oscar was mystified. 'Cowslips?'

Helena jumped to her feet. 'They're a really pretty wild flower that you hardly see any more… I'd love to pick some, but I know how rare they are now. I'm just going to take a closer look.'

Sitting with his legs stretched out in front of him, Oscar leaned back on his elbows watching Helena curiously as she trod carefully between the plants, bending to touch one or two of the flowers tenderly without damaging them. Unlike so many of the worldly women he'd known, it took so little to enchant her, he thought, and so little of her to enchant *him*!

Presently, they got back into the car and set off again, almost immediately coming across a herd of cows lumbering along in the same direction. 'Hmm, this might take some time,' Oscar said mildly, driving carefully behind, giving the herdsman and the two sheepdogs plenty of space.

'I hope Benjamin will let me come with him on his walks with Rosie,' Helena said casually, as they watched the cows being driven into a nearby farm entrance. 'Not having a dog around was one of the things I missed most, living in the city.' She glanced across at

Oscar as she spoke, her eyes taking on a faraway expression as she studied the handsome profile. He was the sort of man that every woman alive would want to be with, she thought. She allowed her eyes to slide downwards for a second, all too aware of the firm, rippling muscles of his thighs beneath his jeans. She swallowed, and stared out of her side window. Dream on, she told herself firmly.

By the time they got to Dorset it was getting quite late. Louise answered Helena's light tap on her door almost at once—obviously relieved that she'd arrived safely—but surprised to see the much larger vehicle there with Oscar sitting at the wheel.

'My car wouldn't start this morning,' Helena explained, 'and luckily for me Oscar was able to come to my rescue.'

'Oh, that was good, then,' Louise said, her shrewd eyes twinkling.

Oscar got out and came over to say hello and Louise opened her door wider. 'Come in...' she began, but Helena shook her head.

'We've got rather a lot to unpack, Louise, thanks,' she said, 'so we'll go on up to the house now.'

'Well, I've left plenty of food—enough for two,' she added, 'and all the bedrooms are ready for occupancy... just as Isobel liked them to be.'

Outside the main entrance to Mulberry Court, Oscar and Helena started unloading, and he glanced down at her.

'Why don't you go and make some tea—I'll do this,' he said.

Helena shot him a grateful look without arguing, and

went to do as he suggested, feeling glad to be home at last. She paused on that thought. *Home?* Yes...glad to be home, she told herself.

In the fridge was one of Louise's famed meat pies. A few minutes in the Aga and that would be delicious, Helena thought happily.

Presently, after he'd had a wash, Oscar joined her. 'I've put a lot of your stuff in your room,' he said, 'but all the books and CDs are in the library.'

Helena smiled quickly. 'Thank you. And while our supper's warming, I'll go and freshen up.'

Upstairs, her cases and bags of clothes and shoes, and the box with her breakables in, were all stacked neatly so that she could reach her bed—which looked so inviting she could collapse into it right now! She'd have plenty of time to unpack after Oscar had gone back, she thought, trying to remember where she'd put her wash bag.

She released her hair from its grip, running her fingers through its long waves. She couldn't find her brush—that would have to do until she shampooed it later, she decided.

When she went back downstairs, Oscar was standing by the window, his hands in his pockets. 'Something smells pretty good,' he said.

'Louise's pies were always wonderful, weren't they?' she said lightly.

After they'd eaten, Helena said, 'When are you due back? When have you booked your return flight?'

'Monday lunch time—but I've a couple of things I need to see to in Dorchester before I return.'

Helena nodded, but said nothing, and after she'd

drunk her glass of white wine from the bottle Louise had left chilling in the fridge, she yawned and got to her feet. 'I suddenly feel desperately in need of a good night's sleep,' she said. She looked down at Oscar. 'Thank you for turning up today,' she said. 'I hope it hasn't inconvenienced you too much.'

He stood up slowly, and Helena's pulse quickened. She hoped this wasn't going to be an action replay of what had happened on that other occasion. Too much had happened already, lately... She could only take so much excitement.

But Oscar moved away, picking up their plates and taking them over to the sink. 'Oh, I never allow myself to be inconvenienced,' he said lazily. 'Anyway, it was in my...our...interests to see that you were safely installed.' He turned to look back at her, a surge of longing hitting his groin. But this was not one of the hot-blooded sisters Allegra, or Callidora, who might have expected him to make love to them tonight; he warned himself. This was Helena, whose heart he had to recapture. And he would succeed, he reassured himself. Timing was everything, and with his usual insight he'd know exactly when the right moment came.

'Goodnight...*Heleena*...' he said softly.

CHAPTER SIX

MID-AFTERNOON next day, with the windscreen wipers going at full throttle, Oscar made his way back to the house. He hadn't intended being so long in Dorchester, but he'd unexpectedly bumped into John Mayhew and had joined him for a drink at The Bear Hotel. There'd been no reply from Helena when he'd texted her to say he'd be late.

Now, he let himself in at the back door fully expecting to see her in the kitchen, but the house was silent and Oscar's lip tilted briefly. She was probably upstairs still unpacking all her clothes, he thought.

He put the kettle on to make himself a coffee, then wandered over to the window… It was dire weather—the rain had been incessant for hours—and Oscar couldn't help feeling slightly nostalgic for the Greek island paradise that he went to whenever he could. It would be fantastic there now, he thought, the incredible blue-green of the sea competing with the brilliance of a cloudless azure sky. When he was there, time became irrelevant.

But this was England, and he knew that weather like today's was fairly normal—though Oscar had to admit that his youthful memories only seemed to conjure up pictures of long, fine days spent here in the lazy countryside.

Suddenly, he saw Benjamin and Rosie coming down from the grounds to the front of the house, and Oscar smiled faintly. They'd obviously been for a very long walk because both man and dog were soaking wet. When Benjamin saw Oscar standing at the window, he raised his hand and mouthed something, before walking rapidly up to the back door. At once Oscar opened it to let him in, but Benjamin stood back.

'Mr Theotokis, would you be kind enough to let Helena know that I've found this crazy animal?' Benjamin said.

'Oh—what happened?' Oscar enquired.

'We were up at the top,' Benjamin said. 'Rosie was sniffing around, good as gold as usual, when suddenly she took off like a rocket and wouldn't come back when I whistled—which isn't like her. I couldn't believe she'd run right off the property like that and go across the road… Well, a couple of roads it turned out to be in the end.' He sighed, blowing out his cheeks. 'When Helena knew the dog had done a runner she insisted on coming with me to help search. She knew where to start looking… Said the local area is known for its rabbit warrens. Then, when we weren't having any luck, we split up and went off in opposite directions—I went west, and she went east.' Benjamin pushed some wet hair from his forehead. 'I was staggered when I found where Rosie had got to… She'd run for miles! I haven't seen Helena since to tell her but it was really good of her to give me some moral support.'

Oscar shrugged. 'I'm not sure that she's back…' he began.

Benjamin cut in quickly, 'Oh, she must be by now!' he exclaimed. 'And we agreed that when either of us found Rosie, we wouldn't try and find each other, we'd just come on home.'

'So—which area were you covering?' Oscar asked, and when Benjamin told him, he nodded. He knew exactly where they would have been. He knew this part of the countryside almost as well as Helena did, even though it was a long time since he'd been around to do any walking.

Presently, after checking that Helena was nowhere in the house, Oscar made himself a coffee, then opened the Sunday newspaper he'd bought, his eyes glancing at the clock on the wall. He shrugged inwardly. She was sure to be back soon, he thought, noting that she hadn't taken her mobile with her because it was there on the table in front of him.

After a while, and not really taking in what he was reading, Oscar made a decision. He put down the paper and went into the utility room, shrugging on the wax jacket he'd hung on the back of the door. Helena had obviously been out for a long time now… He might as well go and meet her, he thought.

Leaving the house, he started trudging up through the grounds. He didn't really know why he was feeling mildly concerned. Although he knew it wouldn't get dark for a long time yet, the clouds were still ominously grey and heavy with rain. Not an ideal day for a woman to be wandering about by herself.

Oscar increased his stride, soon reaching the main

road, then struck out towards the small wooded area where he remembered they used to take Bella for walks sometimes. In the near distance he could see the tree-lined hill that offered a spectacular view from the top, and he decided to make his way up there. Unsurprisingly, there were no other walkers about, he noted, the only significant sounds being the dripping water from the trees and the thrust of his tread on the soaking undergrowth.

At the top of the hill, he cupped his hands around his mouth and called out. 'Helena!' he shouted. *'Heleena!'*

And then he saw her. She was there at the bottom of the field, sitting on a stone stile by a gateway next to the public footpath. She was leaning forward, intent on something, with her head on her knees. Oscar started running down the field, reaching her in a couple of minutes.

She looked up and saw him, a rueful expression on her face. She was wearing a raincoat, but she had nothing on her head and her hair was falling in streaming waves around her face. Her jeans were rolled up to her knees, and her legs and feet were bare and covered in mud.

'Helena…' he began.

She cut in quickly, 'Has Rosie been found?'

Oscar nodded. 'Yes—Benjamin came back with her more than an hour ago but…why on earth are you…?'

Helena grimaced. 'Oh, it's just that I'd completely forgotten about the bog down there at the bottom,' she said, obviously annoyed with herself. 'I was running along and stumbled right into it—and the rain today has made it like glue.' She shuddered. 'Anyway, I was squelching my way through it and I lost my footing and, unfortunately, one of my trainers—which is still stuck down there somewhere.' She leaned back for a second, looking up at him. 'However hard I tried, I could not get it back, and anyway I don't think I'd want it back now. So... I've been trudging along with just one on, and it's very uncomfortable—and cold,' she added, shivering slightly.

Oscar pulled her to her feet. 'Come on,' he said briefly.

Together they made their way slowly back. Oscar had his arm tightly around her waist and Helena leaned against him gratefully, saying 'ouch' once or twice under her breath because her feet were beginning to feel very sore by now and she'd been stung by all the prickles and more than one really cruel nettle. But the only thing she cared about was that the dog had been found.

'I bet I know where Rosie had made for,' she said, glancing up at Oscar. 'After all, it's her job to find things, and this time of year it's an Aladdin's cave to a Retriever.' She paused. 'Poor Benjamin was getting really worried.'

Oscar made no comment, and presently they arrived back at the house.

'I think I need to go up and have a long, hot bath,' Helena said as they hung their wet coats in the utility room. 'Though would you pass me that towel first?' she asked Oscar. 'I can't walk through the house with my feet in this filthy condition.'

'Sit there for a minute,' Oscar commanded, pulling out a wooden stool.

With his back to her, he filled a small bowl with warm water, then took soap and a clean towel and knelt down in front of Helena. He paused for a second, then looked up at her slowly, a quizzical expression in his eyes, and in spite of this most unpromising romantic scenario, Helena felt a tremor of sexual excitement ripple through her. She knew she was looking dreadful, her hair in soaking wet waves around her mud-spattered face—yet Oscar's penetrating gaze made her feel utterly feminine, utterly desirable. A heated flush stained her cheeks as their eyes met.

Slowly, he began soaping her feet, one at a time, moving his fingers carefully over each toe. Then his strong brown hands began massaging the calves of her legs, behind her knees, moving down to cup her heels in his palms, moving rhythmically, his touch reaching every part of her bare flesh, and with her head dropped back and her eyes half-closed in pure ecstasy, Helena gave a long sigh of uninhibited pleasure. She could not remember a time in her life when anyone had bathed her—even partially, or touched her in the way that Oscar was doing—and it was making her feel guilty to be revelling in the sensuous experience.

'Oh…that feels…so…lovely…' she murmured.

After a few blissful moments she opened her eyes to see him looking at her with that dangerous, penetrating gaze that had always reduced her to helplessness. What he was doing to her was going far beyond the call of duty, she thought—but she didn't want it to stop! Wanted it to go on and on!

Finally, Oscar lifted her feet from the bowl and began to dry them carefully, his dark head bent to the task, his manipulating, sensitive fingers continuing far longer than was necessary because he knew that she was enjoying the warmth of his hands, the erotic pressure of his touch that might easily lead to something far more. He allowed himself a wry inward smile. He had never made love to a woman in such surroundings... but he was all too aware that place was unimportant as long as the chemistry was there. And he knew that he and Helena had enough chemistry between them to last them two lifetimes.

Alerted to the strength of feeling that had developed between them, Helena got up quickly, a familiar, persistent warning bell bringing an end to her passionate reverie. 'Thanks...thanks...that's OK—that's fine,' she said. As she made for the door she turned to look back at him. 'I'll make supper for us in an hour or so,' she said.

Much later, as they sat in the conservatory with their coffee, Oscar said casually, 'I bought you a car this morning, Helena.'

Helena frowned, looking up at him quickly. 'What do you mean?'

'I bought you a car,' he repeated. Before she could say anything, he went on, 'It occurred to me that you're going to need transport for the time you're here, and I've a contact in one of the garages in the town who was able to sort it out quickly for me.' Oscar drank from his cup. 'It's registered in your name and they'll be delivering it tomorrow morning—it's the newest model of the one you've been driving,' he added.

Helena could hardly believe what she'd heard, and she felt mildly irritated. He'd done what? She did not want Oscar buying her expensive things, she thought. She'd already told him she had enough money of her own for now—but it did not include the possibility of purchasing new cars! She'd never owned a brand new car in her life! That huge expense would have to wait until…well, until next year.

'Oscar, I'm not ready to buy a car yet,' she said firmly.

'You haven't bought it—I have,' he said. Then, seeing the expression on Helena's face, he said coolly, 'We can call it the Mulberry Court car if you prefer, purely for present, temporary use. And I was not expecting any financial input from you,' he added bluntly.

Helena shook her head briefly. Spending big money so casually was nothing to Oscar—which only showed the huge difference between them, she thought. The difference that could never be breached. Then something else struck her—perhaps this was him attempting to 'buy her out' of their inheritance? To persuade her to take the money and run? As she knew he wanted her to.

Feeling slightly guilty at that uncharitable thought, Helena put it out of her mind at once. Buying the car had been generous—and thoughtful—of him, though if it had been left up to her she'd have merely hired one. That would have been sufficient for the short time involved.

For a few moments there was an uneasy silence between them, Oscar sensing that Helena wasn't particularly happy. Well, she'd had a very long and wet walk today, and had obviously been anxious about the dog… He glanced at his watch, getting up suddenly.

'I've just remembered that I've left something I need in the car,' he said briefly, leaving the room.

Helena got up and went over to the window, her mind still fixed on those moments when Oscar had bathed her feet. Even now, her thighs tingled at the memory. Why had no other man ever been able to raise her to such sensual heights? And with such ease? And was her unsatisfactory experience in other relationships all because of Oscar? Was she always chasing an impossible dream—*their* impossible dream? And would no other dream, no other man do?

Helena frowned at all this introspection. It was foolish to ask herself these questions, she told herself.

Just then the mobile phone on the table rang and, without thinking, she turned to answer it. And, too late, she realized it was Oscar's mobile which she'd automatically picked up.

'Hello?' she said uncertainly, glancing towards the door.

The voice on the other end was female. 'Oh... Oh, hello?... Hello?' Then, 'Who is this, please? I wish to speak to Oscar Theotokis.'

'Um...well, he'll be here in a moment,' Helena said. Then, 'Can I give him a message?'

After a brief pause, the voice said—in a rather heavy, imperious tone, 'Yes...why not?' She continued speaking in English, but with a heavily laced accent. 'Tell him that, most unfortunately, my sister Allegra has lost her baby...again.' Silence, then a long sigh before the woman continued. 'I know that Oscar will want to know that,' she added. 'Tell him, also, that I would like to speak to him soon... This is Callidora speaking.'

Helena swallowed over a dry tongue. 'Look...um... I'm sure he will be back in a moment,' she said, 'if you'll just hang on...'

'No—I have to go. Please make sure he gets this message.' And with that, the phone went dead.

Helena put the mobile back down on the table, wishing with all her heart that she hadn't answered it. It had been an instinctive act on her part to do so, but the call had obviously been a very personal one, and she'd rather not have known about it. She stared down at the instrument as if hoping it might reveal more information. So this woman—Allegra—had lost her baby, the caller had said—and it seemed important that Oscar knew about it...

Helena shook her head briefly and began putting their coffee things on to the tray just as Oscar returned carrying a large file. Without looking at him, she said, 'I just answered your mobile—sorry—I should have let it ring.' She reached for the small cream jug and put it down carefully with the mugs. 'It was someone—a lady—Callidora...and she rang to let you know that her sister has just lost her baby. And also that she would like to speak to you—soon.'

Now Helena did look up at Oscar, horribly conscious of the dark, unfathomable expression in his eyes—and unable to ignore the sinking of her own heart.

'Oh...I see,' was all he said casually, taking the tray from Helena and going out before her to the kitchen. 'Did you tell Callidora that I would be back in Greece tomorrow?' he added.

'I didn't tell her anything,' Helena said.

Presently, up in her bedroom, Helen undressed

slowly and got ready for bed. She had been plunged from a sense of unbelievable pleasure and well-being to feeling acutely depressed. Depressed and insecure.

Because there was so much she knew about Oscar— and so much she didn't know. Not any more. Nor was she ever likely to know.

At around midnight, Oscar came up the stairs to bed. More than anything in the world, he wanted to make love to Helena. Now. And it wasn't just romantic passion that was torturing him. He longed to hold her close to him, to protect her… She had looked so defenceless down in that field earlier in the day, so unutterably vulnerable. So hotly desirable. And there had been a few moments, later, as he'd dried her toes, when he'd recognized that special look in her magical eyes that had told him all he needed to know.

Going past his own room, he walked softly towards Helena's door and stood for a moment, listening. The only sound he could hear was her gentle breathing, and very carefully he opened the door just wide enough to look inside.

She was lying on her back on the bed, one slim leg carelessly over the side, her arms raised above her, her hair fanning out loosely on the pillow. She still had her underwear on, the rest of her clothes and the duvet were scattered on the floor beside her.

Unable to resist going closer, Oscar went inside and stood looking down. She was deeply asleep, a pale moon reflecting light on the skin of her slender neck, on the rounded curve of her naked thigh. Her long eyelashes swept her cheeks, her lips were slightly parted, her breasts in the lacy bra rising and falling gently with each breath.

With his blood rushing and almost overcome with need, Oscar swallowed hard, then stooped to pick up the duvet. Very carefully, he placed it over her, gathering the folds up around her neck, tucking them in gently. He paused for only a second before turning to leave.

'*Kalinihta, agapi mou,*' he whispered.

CHAPTER SEVEN

ON MONDAY morning the new silver-blue car arrived and, although Helena had felt annoyed at Oscar taking what she saw as an unnecessary step in buying it for her, she had to admit to a feeling of pride as she drove it for the first time. And, of course, he had been right. She was obviously going to need some form of transport while she was here, either to go into Dorchester for fresh supplies or, more importantly, to get her to any future job she may have to find. Helena frowned as she remembered her feeling of hopelessness at not being able to drive away on Saturday afternoon and she also remembered how she'd felt when she awoke to find Oscar's quizzical eyes gazing at her through the open window. It was a huge stroke of luck that he'd happened to be in the UK, she thought—had her guardian angel been at work again?

By the end of the week, Helena had settled into Mulberry Court with no problem. Louise popped up to the house fairly frequently, to do the sort of tasks she normally did, and Helena enjoyed helping her sometimes—and chatting about the past.

But what was mostly on Helena's mind was listing all the valuable contents of the house. Although she'd been aware of Oscar taking some notes the other day, she wanted to catalogue everything herself—for her own satisfaction—and to start thinking about eventually taking some of it away with her, even though that thought made her shudder. It was here, in this house, where everything truly belonged, not split up and sold off—it would almost feel like vandalism. But she had to be realistic, she realized that. Quite apart from her figurines, which she kept peeping in to look at, there was so much expensive stuff here and it all had to go somewhere. And as for the library with hundreds of Isobel's books, she thought, looking around her now... A lot of them would find their way into her new home—wherever that turned out to be.

She looked pensively out of the window for a moment. She'd have to find that special job in London first, then probably rent somewhere on a short-term let while she looked around for a permanent home. But she wouldn't know what to look for until she knew what her resources might be... Until they sold Mulberry Court next year.

She bit her lip. She did not want to think about the financial aspect of all this, had deliberately shut her mind to it until the day came. Being here, now, was all she needed because, apart from the cottage she'd shared with her father all those years ago, this was the place she would always think of as home. It always made her feel so comfortable, so welcome, so wanted. And she certainly felt no anxiety at the thought of sleeping here by herself, as Oscar had thought she might.

She'd received numerous calls from him since he'd gone back, which was something of a surprise. Now that he knew she was keeping potential squatters at bay and that she'd settled in, surely there was no need for him to keep checking up? But she freely admitted that she looked forward to hearing from him, hearing his voice, and yesterday he'd said he was making arrangements to come back to the UK, probably within a few days. Helena hugged herself as she thought of that. Although she knew that her renewed feelings for Oscar were causing her to tread on dangerous ground, it couldn't do any harm to enjoy being with him again for just the brief interlude which fate had decreed. It didn't have to mean anything to her—not anything serious, she assured herself. In fact, she'd make sure it didn't. She'd grown up in the last ten years, had taken a few knocks and was quite ready for a few more if that was what life decided. Until then, it wasn't a crime to enjoy being in the company of the most handsome man on God's earth, was it? The only 'crime' would be if she let herself get carried away. And she would not let that happen this time. She was going to just live for the moment.

Helena was in the utility room putting some of her clothes into the washing machine when Louise came in, obviously concerned about something and in a somewhat breathless state.

'Helena…I've just had a phone call from Sarah, my cousin—and it's not good news.'

Helena looked up quickly. 'Oh—what's happened, Louise?'

'She's just rung me now, from the hospital…she's suffered a detached retina, poor thing. It happened all of a sudden, apparently, They operated last night, and she expects to be home on Monday, all being well. But the thing is—she's going to need someone to look after her for a week or so because she won't be able to see for a while. And, quite honestly, I'm the only one available…I'm her only relation, you see. Sarah's very proud. She won't want to leave it up to neighbours, even though they're all very kind.' Louise frowned anxiously.

'So when are you going—and have you found out the train times? I can drive you to the station,' Helena said at once.

They went into the kitchen, and Louise sat at the table for a moment, looking up at Helena. 'There's a train at ten-thirty in the morning,' she said, 'but…I feel really upset at having to go, because it means I won't be with you, Helena… It's so nice having you down here again. It's like old times.' She frowned anxiously. 'And of course I can't say exactly when I'll be back. It'll all depend how I find things at Durham, and how well Sarah is going to recover. Everything takes that bit longer as you get older,' she added. 'But I'm going to really hate missing out being here with you, Helena.'

'Oh, these things happen, Louise,' Helena said kindly. 'And don't worry—I'm not returning to London just yet. You're sure to come home before I do. And, in the meantime, Sarah needs you, so you must go.' Helena went over to put the kettle on. 'I'll bring the car down to the cottage at nine forty-five, shall I. That'll give us plenty of time to get to the station,' she added, thinking that Oscar had been right in buying the car, after all.

'The other thing that's a bit unfortunate is that this weekend Benjamin won't be here, either. He's going to spend some time with his children—which doesn't happen very frequently,' Louise said, watching as Helena put out two mugs for the coffee she was making for them. 'His ex-wife always makes it so difficult for him, and he's such a good man, so reliable and kind,' Louise added. She looked thoughtful for a second.

Helena nodded in agreement. 'Oscar told me all about what happened to him,' she added.

After a moment Louise said, shooting a glance at Helena, 'Seeing Mr Oscar again is quite something, isn't it?' She paused. 'Of course, he didn't visit Isobel that much of late, but she knew the reason for that... She often mentioned his very responsible job, the long hours he has to work. But he was often around in the old days, when you were both youngsters, wasn't he?' she added.

'Yes, he was always here for his holidays,' Helena said casually. 'I haven't seen anything of him since, and of course the only reason for him being about now is because of the will.' She brought the coffee over to the table and sat down, and Louise stirred hers slowly, watching the liquid swirl around in the mug.

'Life's a funny old thing, isn't it, when you think about it,' Louise said. 'You never know how it's going to turn out, or what's going to turn up next.'

Helena could only nod in agreement.

At around midnight on Sunday, something—and she could not identify what it was—made Helena wake up and sit bolt upright in bed, her heart gathering pace.

What *was* it she had heard that had brought her rapidly from a deep sleep to an alert wakefulness?

She stayed quite still for a moment, then slipped from beneath her duvet and went across to look out of the window. Nothing. Only the whispering of a light breeze ruffling the leaves on the trees, the pale moon overhead half-shrouded by cotton wool clouds causing dark shadows to filter in and out of the night. But... something was different... Something had brought Helena swiftly to a state of tense alertness, and she knew she wouldn't get back to sleep until she'd gone to have a look around.

She dragged on her dressing gown, a sudden instinct making her pause to take her mobile from her bag. Then, bare-foot, she left the room and went downstairs, treading silently along the hall. Hesitating, she pulled herself up for a moment. There it was again...and she knew now! It was coughing that she'd heard. Someone was coughing, someone was choking, and there was whispering... Then another smothered wheezy cough.

Although momentarily rooted to the spot, Helena didn't feel frightened—and afterwards she would ask herself why she hadn't been. She went into the kitchen and over to the window and stared out, the house security lights illuminating the scene all around.

Two men were there, wearing dark hoodies, one of them bigger than the other. They were crouching forward, attempting to force the back door to gain entry, totally intent on what they were doing.

By now, Helena's tongue had dried and her pulse was racing, yet despite that she knew she was feeling amazingly calm, almost detached. It was like watch-

ing a scene being played out in front of her, she thought
fleetingly. Then she saw one of them push the hood
away from his face and she frowned, peering to take
a closer look. This was not a *man*, she saw at once; it
was a young boy with pale unshaven features, and he
was in the midst of a very bad asthma attack. Helena
recognized it at once because Jason had been a suf-
ferer, too.

Relaxing her tense shoulders and as if in sympathy,
Helena drew in her own breath deeply, then stepped
forward and released both inside locks, throwing the
door open wide.

'Allow me to save you the trouble, gentlemen,' she
said pleasantly. 'What is it you want?'

Driving rapidly in the direction of Mulberry Court,
Oscar's expression was dark, the thought of what might
have happened to Helena sending icy shivers right
down his spine. It had certainly been enough to bring
him back from Greece at the earliest possible moment.

Three days earlier he'd learned from Helena that
Louise had gone to Durham to look after her cousin,
and then Helena had added, almost airily, that there'd
been night-time intruders at the house. Which, for once
in his life, had left Oscar speechless.

He'd pressed her for details, but Helena had refused
to elaborate, saying that it had all been dealt with. But
that hadn't satisfied Oscar and he couldn't wait to return and find out more—and convince himself that
Helena was all right, that nothing bad had happened
to her.

Now, it was Wednesday evening as he drew up to

the entrance of Mulberry Court. As he got out of the car, Helena opened the front door to greet him, smiling brightly.

She was wearing a long, swirly black skirt almost down to her toes, teamed with a flimsy peasant-style top, and she'd brushed her hair out loose so that it fell halfway down her back. Oscar stared down at her, his eyes forbiddingly dark. Her small stature made her look so defenceless as she stood framed in the doorway and he gritted his teeth. It hadn't been such a good idea for her to stay here by herself, he thought, even though it had been what she wanted.

'Hi,' she said carelessly. 'Good flight?' With a slightly sinking heart, Helena recognized that familiar brooding look on his face. She knew that she was going to have to face an inquisition about Sunday night. Maybe she *should* have acted differently, she thought. What if, thanks to her, the place had been ransacked, all the valuable contents whisked away, never to be seen again? That possibility would obviously be the most important thing on Oscar's mind when she eventually tried to explain.

With only a brief response to her enquiry, Oscar went up the stairs carrying his large luggage holdall and business equipment. In his room, he washed the dust of the journey from his hands and face, then took a clean shirt from his case. He'd brought enough of everything with him to stay much longer this time—to stay as long as it took—and work would carry on much as usual, thanks to the current high-class technology at his disposal. But, for once, he had much more personal things on his mind… For once, he was not putting the company first.

Presently, down in the kitchen, he watched as Helena prepared the supper she'd said she would be making for them. Reluctantly tearing his gaze away from her, he glanced around him briefly. He was tired, and suddenly the long cushioned sofa at one end of the room seemed particularly inviting.

The scrubbed wooden table was set with two places and there was a jug of water and a bottle of wine. As Helena brought over a large serving dish from the oven, she said lightly, 'Although I've watched Louise do enough cooking here over the years, I obviously had no reason to do much of it myself.' She smiled up at Oscar quickly. 'I hope you approve of gammon cutlets with pineapple and salad…and our own little new potatoes which Benjamin dug for us this morning.'

She put the rest of the meal in front of them, then sat down. 'I've really enjoyed preparing it,' she added.

Oscar pulled out his own chair and sat down. 'It all looks…excellent…Helena,' he said briefly. 'Thank you.'

As she carefully passed the plate to Oscar, it was impossible for Helena to ignore the somewhat uneasy atmosphere in the room as they made desultory conversation. As she helped herself to one or two of the buttery potatoes, she gave him a sidelong glance—and realized that he'd been looking at her. She looked away again. Then, 'I wonder just who will be sitting here next year,' she said. 'They're going to be very lucky, whoever they are.' She paused for a moment, putting down her fork. 'I hope they turn out to be nice people…I mean, people worthy of Mulberry Court. I hate to think of strangers taking over…it's going to feel all wrong—and they'll never love it as we do,' she added.

They ate in silence for a few moments, then Oscar said, without looking at her, 'Now, you're going to tell me *exactly* what happened here the other night, Helena.'

Well, she'd been waiting for the interrogation, she thought, so she'd better get it over with. She finished her meal, then stood up and went over to make the coffee.

'It was nothing—not really—' she began over her shoulder.

Before she could go on he interrupted harshly, 'It was not "nothing", *Heleena!* It was something…' and, trembling slightly, Helena heard the tantalizing, marked inflexion of his mother tongue, the sound that always made her weak at the knees. 'I cannot bring myself to believe that you handled it yourself, that you didn't call the police when you knew intruders were trying to gain entry to Mulberry Court! What on earth were you thinking?' He almost spat out the words.

Steadying her hand as she finished making the coffee, Helena said calmly, 'Well, where would you like me to begin, Oscar?'

'At the beginning—naturally,' he said dryly.

There was silence for a few moments, then, pouring the coffee into two mugs, she brought the tray over to the table and sat down.

'That night, something made me wake up. I can't remember the time, but it was very late—or very early—and I knew I had to go down and find out what it was.'

She looked across at him defiantly. 'I wasn't frightened. I was—well—curious, that's all.'

Oscar's eyes were locked on to hers, but he said nothing as she continued.

'When I peeped out of the kitchen window I saw two...two men, I thought...and they were trying to fit a key into the door lock. They were whispering, and one of them was coughing and gasping for breath—and that's what had woken me up. It was a horrible sound,' she added, and as Oscar was about to speak she went on quickly. 'I had to do something so I opened the door, because I suddenly realized that these were not men at all, they were *kids*...a couple of kids...and when they came inside I could see that one of them was in a seriously bad way.'

Oscar's eyebrows shot up. 'You actually...*invited*... them *in*? he asked incredulously.

'Of course I did—' Helena began, and he interrupted.

'*Ya to onoma tou Theiou!*' he exclaimed, lapsing into a spontaneous and very rare expletive. 'You should have called the police straight away!'

'What a waste of public money *that* would have turned out to be!' Helena retorted. 'Anyway, I might have done if I'd seen a couple of gangsters wielding baseball bats but they weren't even trying to break down the door, or cause any damage... They just had a random handful of keys, hoping one of them would fit. And such was their "street wisdom" it didn't seem to occur to them that there might be bolts on the inside,' she added, smiling faintly.

'I don't know what you find so amusing,' Oscar said

bluntly. 'They might have been kids, as you say, but they were tall enough for you not to realize that at first and there were two of them and one of you. They could have overpowered you and vandalised the place.' He shook his head as if he could not believe what Helena was telling him. Wasn't part of her reason for staying here to look after Mulberry Court? Surely that didn't include welcoming in random burglars!

'Why on earth didn't you think to ring Benjamin?' he demanded. 'He would have come straight up, whatever time it was.'

'Because,' Helena said, 'Benjamin was away visiting his children.'

At this piece of news, Oscar glowered visibly. So, Helena had been here, totally alone, with no one near enough to be of assistance. His mouth set in a determined line. He'd make sure that she was never in that position again, he told himself.

'Anyway—' Helena took another sip of her coffee '—I made them tell me what they thought they were doing. Apparently, they'd told their mother they were having a sleepover at a friend's house, but what they'd really wanted was to sleep out rough to see what it was like, I suppose—it's "cool". But when it began to get cold, Harry, the younger one—he's only twelve—succumbed to one of his rare asthma attacks and they both got frightened.'

'Why didn't they just go home?' Oscar demanded.

'They couldn't do that! They said their mother would kill them when she found out what they'd been up to!'

'But what made them come *here*? I suppose it couldn't have had anything to do with the fact that they knew the place was empty—or they thought it was,' Oscar suggested scornfully. 'Where they could break in uninterrupted.'

'It was not like that at all,' Helena said, knowing that her colour was rising with every word Oscar was saying. 'Mulberry Court is well-known to the boys,' she went on. 'They'd been here carol singing and trick-or-treating…and apparently Isobel would invite them in every time—and their friends as well.' Helena paused, adding quietly, 'They said they knew Mrs Theotokis had died but that she would have let them in if she'd been here.'

There was silence for a few moments, then Helena said, 'Isobel always took people on trust. That's why everyone loved her.'

Taking people on trust is all very well—up to a point, Oscar thought tightly. But he decided to let that pass.

'So, after you'd made your…assessment…of the situation,' Oscar said, his mouth still set in an obstinate line, 'what happened after that?'

'I made them cosy for the rest of the night, and…'

'You did *what*? You mean—they *slept* here?' Oscar demanded.

'Yes—eventually—after I'd calmed Harry down and made sure his breathing had improved,' she said. 'Then I made them some hot chocolate.' Helena paused. 'They were nice lads,' she added thoughtfully.

'So, where did they actually sleep?' Oscar asked, realizing that this was a battle he was never going to win.

'Don't worry—not in your bed, or mine,' Helena

said. 'I brought down a couple of duvets and made Harry comfy on the sofa over there, and then I put cushions from the conservatory on the floor next to him for Caleb.' She met Oscar's gaze levelly. 'They were asleep in less than five minutes, and I had to wake them up in the morning,' she added.

'But how can you be sure they didn't steal something?' Oscar demanded, still not willing to admit defeat.

Helena sighed with exasperation. 'Oscar, when they were awake I was with them all the time—apart from the few moments while I went to fetch the duvets.' She looked at him quickly. That was what had worried Oscar, she thought. That some of their valuable belongings might have disappeared. 'I promise you,' she said tightly, 'not a single teaspoon is missing.'

For a few moments they looked at each other in silent combat.

'And at what time did they vacate the premises?' Oscar asked.

'I had to wake them at eight o'clock, and after I'd sent them along to the wet room for a wash, I made them tea and toast.' Helena shrugged. 'I did give them a gentle lecture before sending them on their way.' She smiled, remembering something. 'And as they left, they both looked at me seriously and said, "Thank you for having us." Wasn't that sweet?' Helena said.

Oscar gazed at her, his thoughts in turmoil. Of course Helena was right—as it happened, she had not been in any danger, this time. But it would have been so different if the intruders had been different people...

He didn't want to think of what could have happened to her…

'And what about you… Did you get any sleep at all during that night?' he said at last.

Helena shook her head briefly. 'No, I was wide awake—and, anyway, I thought it best not to go to sleep, so I made myself comfortable in the sitting room. I had the TV on very quietly,' she added.

'Better not to disturb the guests,' Oscar said, trying not to sound too cynical.

'Quite. It's what Isobel would have expected,' Helena said neatly.

Suddenly, Oscar leaned forward and filled both their glasses with wine. 'I don't know how long you expect to stay here for your short…sabbatical…Helena, but I've actually made arrangements to stay longer myself this time.' When Helena went to say something, he went on quickly, 'The fact that Louise is not going to be around for some while does change things.'

'I'll be perfectly OK here without Louise to hold my hand, Oscar!' Helena exclaimed. 'And Benjamin's always—well, usually—around. Surely you haven't the time to waste on me!'

She looked at him defiantly…before the more obvious point struck her. He wasn't thinking of *her* welfare—he was thinking about Mulberry Court. And he was clearly of the opinion that she couldn't be trusted to take care of it without him there.

'I won't be wasting any time,' Oscar said calmly. 'I shall be working each day in the study.'

As well as making a rather more personal plan, he thought, which was to get Helena away from here. Just for a few days. Away from Mulberry Court, where there were too many memories, too much emotional baggage. Too much 'stuff' getting in his way.

He knew there was a lot of ground to be made up, and he knew how he was going to do that best. And soon.

By making love to Helena under the seductive influence of an azure Mediterranean sky.

CHAPTER EIGHT

MUCH later that night as he was preparing for bed, Oscar kept going over and over everything Helena had told him. He still found it hard to believe that she would have opened the door to those men—boys—it didn't matter which. She would have been no match for them. And it had had to take place on the very rare occasion when no one had been at the cottages. When there would have been absolutely no one to come to her aid. He didn't want to go on thinking of the possibilities. Of what might have been.

He stood thoughtfully under the shower for a few minutes, then, with a white towel slung around his tanned shoulders, he padded naked and barefoot over to the bed, rubbing briskly at his wet hair with the corner of the huge towel. He was going to have to convince Helena that a few days away in hot sunshine might compare favourably with the rather damp conditions which Dorset was having at the moment. He'd pick his moment to suggest it. But it would happen. He'd make sure it would happen.

He was about to flop down on the bed when a sound outside made him stop and turn to listen. Someone was talking—well, whispering—someone was out there...

Grabbing the towel and tying it around his waist, Oscar reached his door in a few strides and opened it to see Helena, wearing a short, flimsy nightdress, her hair in total disarray, move slowly past. Her eyes were shut tightly, her lips forming inaudible words. Treading as if her feet were hardly touching the ground, she reached the top of the staircase. Realizing at once what was happening, Oscar went over to her silently, automatically slipping his arm around her protectively.

Unaware that anyone was beside her, Helena took each step down, one at a time, like a child learning to walk, and now, with his head close to hers, Oscar could make out what she was whispering.

'My figurines…I want to see if they've taken my figurines…' Her voice was breathy, fragile as, with her hand on the banister, she continued her dream-state walk. 'Isobel said they were mine, that's all I wanted… I never wanted anything else at all. And now the boys might have taken them…they might have taken them away…I must go and see…I must try to find them, to get them back.'

Desperately trying not to frighten her into wakefulness, Oscar said very gently, 'It's all right…the figurines are still in the library, Helena, where they've always been…no one has taken them, I promise you.'

They reached the bottom of the stairs and, still with her eyes closed, Helena said, her voice quivering, 'Are you sure they're safe? The boys didn't steal them, did they…?'

'No, they didn't. They're quite safe, Helena.'

Helena smiled a sweet, childlike smile. 'Of course… I knew Isobel would look after them for me.'

She turned around slowly. 'I'm glad the boys didn't take them,' she said, her head lolling down on her chest.

Quietly, carefully, with Oscar half-carrying her, the two made the return journey up the stairs and into Helena's bedroom. Oscar helped her get into bed and covered her up, waiting for her to stir or say something else. But by now she was in a deep sleep, her breathing easy, her expression one of pure contentment as she lay there, and to Oscar she looked like a pale goddess in the half-light.

Feeling as if he, himself, had been in some kind of dream, he stood watching her for several minutes, loving the enchanting sight of her, not wanting to leave her. Then, bending, he kissed her forehead lightly and left the room.

Next morning, it was gone nine o'clock before Helena awoke and she sat up, her shoulders drooping. She was feeling as tired as if she hadn't slept a wink, she thought dismally, her head feeling distinctly woolly, giving her a sense of being detached from her brain. She knew that she'd been dreaming all night—and it was all to do with that telephone call from 'Callidora', that message about the lost baby.

She climbed out of bed and went into the bathroom, and the mirror told its own story as she stared at her reflection. Her eyes looked huge in a pale face which showed evidence of silent tears being shed as she'd been sleeping…

Shaking herself properly awake, Helena switched the shower on to hot, then, as she let the water stream over her hair and body, she couldn't resist trying to catch some of the fast disappearing moments of her night's restless sleep. It was like trying to pick up quicksilver in her fingers, she thought, as she struggled to reclaim the mental picture that was uppermost, the dream she was desperate not to lose. And then, quite clearly, it came back to her. The moment that she'd watched herself walking up the aisle on her father's arm.

Oscar had been standing at the altar. He'd turned to greet her as she'd approached, and her heart had almost burst with love as their eyes had met. Her dainty straight white cotton dress was trimmed with a delicate lace edging, her hair piled on top and held in place by a single white rose, matching the small spray she was carrying and which she'd picked from the garden that morning.

But then, with a horrible sickening twist, a woman appeared from nowhere. And she was carrying a baby—a baby which Oscar took and held close to him…

Annoyed with herself for feeling so upset by recalling the dream—the stupid, pointless dream—Helena got out of the shower and dried herself, doubly certain, now, of something she'd always known. Her life-long love for Oscar had no future. And Mulberry Court didn't belong to her, despite the terms of the will. From the very beginning, her world and Oscar's had been so far apart they might just as well have been born on different planets. And so much time had passed since they'd been so close—so much time he would obviously have spent in the company of many, many women.

She finished getting dressed and reached for her hairbrush. She could hardly bear to wait for the sale of the house now, she thought, dragging her hair back and pushing it haphazardly into some sort of order. Her connection with Mulberry Court would eventually reach a conclusion, and when it did she would rethink her career and start all over again.

And as for the money she'd receive from Isobel's estate, which had always felt wrong and undeserved, well, she'd put that safely away with what her father had left her, she decided.

She hadn't heard a sound from Oscar that morning, and when she went down into the kitchen there was a note on the table. *Gone to Dorchester. Back later. O.*

Helena shrugged, and put the kettle on to make herself some tea. And as soon as she'd had breakfast, she thought, she'd find Benjamin and perhaps they could go for a walk with the dog.

Helena was just about to leave the house when the doorbell rang, and she raised her eyes. That couldn't be Benjamin because he always tapped on the back door, and Oscar had his own key…

She went quickly along the hall and opened the door. A young, very pretty dark-haired woman stood there, two small boys at her side.

'Mrs Theotokis?' she asked uncertainly, and before Helena could reply, she said, 'I'm sorry to bother you… but is he…is Mr Theotokis at home?' The accent was foreign, cultured.

Helena stood back, feeling awkward for a second. 'Um, no…I'm afraid he's not,' she said. 'But can I help?'

The woman shook her head briefly. 'No, I don't think so, thank you.' She paused. 'I want to speak to Mr Theotokis myself…face to face…so I'd be grateful if you could let me know if and when he might be available.' And, seeing the confused expression on Helena's face, she added, 'It won't take long, but the children would like to see him. And it's…it's very important that they do.'

Helena's gaze rested on the boys for a moment. They were such beautiful children, clear-eyed, dark-skinned and with lustrous black hair. Who was this woman, and who were these children? she asked herself. She found her voice at last.

'I'm not sure when…when Mr Theotokis will be back, but can I give him a message?' she asked.

The woman thought for a moment, then, 'No, this is something far too personal, I'm afraid,' she said. 'And not something that can be said by proxy. But don't worry, I'll make sure that I catch up with him at some point.' She reached into her handbag and took out a large envelope. 'In the meantime, would you be kind enough to give him this?' She hesitated. 'We've been here on an extended holiday, but we're flying back home this afternoon so time is short, I'm afraid.' She held out her hand to shake Helena's. 'Well, goodbye— and I'm sorry to have bothered you.'

And with that she turned to go. With her frown deepening, Helena watched them walk away towards a waiting taxi at the end of the drive, the children casting backward glances at her as they went.

Later, in the library, Helena opened the windows wide, letting the spring air bring in a delicate scent of new growth to tease her nostrils, and she took a deep breath. Then a sudden shaft of sunlight picked out the alcove where her shepherd and shepherdess stood, where they had been standing for as long as Helena could remember. She went over to look down at them again.

The creator of those exquisite porcelain figures had breathed life, real life, into them, she thought, had given them feelings which could be interpreted by anyone taking the time to just stand and stare for a few moments. The caring, manly stance of the shepherd, and the gentle tilt of his head, indicated the purest form of true love for the lady he was gazing down at so adoringly—and the expression on the dainty features of his shepherdess was so touching it made a lump form in Helena's throat. She swallowed. Why hadn't she noticed all that before? she asked herself. Had it been there all this time, or was she just feeling extra-sensitive today?

Drawing her attention away from the love scene she had unwittingly stumbled upon, Helena looked up to see Isobel's eyes searching for hers and she went across to stand beneath the portrait for a moment. Apart from her figurines, she thought, she would ask Oscar if she could have the portrait too, so that wherever Helena's next home turned out to be, Isobel would have pride of place there.

Much later, Oscar returned. Helena was in the conservatory reading her book. He glanced down at her. She was wearing a simple cream cotton dress and strappy sandals, her shoulder-skimming hair tied loosely. He cleared his throat.

'I happened to meet John Mayhew in town this morning,' he said.

Helena didn't look up. 'Oh?'

'He told me he's been approached about the sale of Mulberry Court. Apparently Amethyst Trust Hotels want to buy it, so that they can convert it. They want to build a spa, treatment rooms, a conference centre and swimming pool.' Oscar went across to the window, looking out. He paused before going on. 'They feel it would be a perfect site for such a development, with the unusually extensive grounds and garden, all of which would be completely swallowed up, of course. In fact, if they have their way, Mulberry Court as it is now would be wiped off the map for ever,' he added, keeping his voice deliberately cool.

Now Helena did look up, a frown pleating her forehead. 'Well, I hope John Mayhew told them that the house is not up for sale...not yet, anyway,' she said.

'Oh, they know that,' Oscar said. 'But these people are all about forward planning. They wouldn't care how long it took, just so long as they got it in the end. Apparently, the local Planning Department have already been informally approached and have given Amethyst sufficient optimism to think that such a project could go through. Assuming, of course, the all-important matter of first acquiring the land,' he added.

Helena snapped her book shut and stood up. 'Well, *assuming* that I...we...have the sole responsibility of selling Mulberry Court to the *right* owner,' she said, 'you can tell John Mayhew that Amethyst whoever-they-are can get lost. I would never, never agree to sell to such people!'

Oscar couldn't help smiling at Helena's obvious aggravation at what he'd just told her. And he'd known what her reaction would be. He put out his hand to halt her progress as she went to go past him. 'We don't need to worry about any of that yet,' he said soothingly, 'but John was quite right to keep us informed.'

'I suppose so,' Helena said reluctantly. Then, 'Oh...' She began, sneezing into her hand, and Oscar immediately reached into his pocket and passed her a handkerchief. Helena took it from him. 'Oh, dear, that's the third time I've done that...I think I'm getting a cold,' she sniffed, dabbing furiously. 'My throat felt suspiciously sore when I woke up this morning.'

'Hardly a surprise,' Oscar said mildly, 'considering the wet weather you've been experiencing here lately...' He stood up. 'And that's why there's something else I need to tell you. I'm making arrangements for us to have a short holiday,' he said. 'You need a dose of real sunshine, Helena.'

Helena looked up at him. 'What do you mean... What sort of holiday?' she mumbled through the large handkerchief, which was almost covering her face.

'To Greece...or to my island getaway, I should say,' Oscar said.

'But...what about leaving Mulberry Court empty? Aren't you worried about someone gaining entry?' Helena asked.

'Oh, the house will look after itself for the few days I have in mind,' Oscar said evenly. 'And this time we'll make sure that Benjamin's around, in any case.'

Helena stared at him, biting her lip. Although she'd always longed to visit Oscar's homeland—and he'd always promised her that one day she would—now she wasn't sure she wanted to, at least not with him. Wouldn't it be helping to prolong something which could only end in more heartache? Relaxing in the sun, bathing in a warm sea...having nothing to think about except enjoying long, lazy moments—a heady, dangerous cocktail. 'I'll have to think about it,' she said. 'I have things to do here, and I'm not really sure whether...whether I want to go.'

Oscar went before her towards the door, then looked back, his dark eyebrows slightly raised. 'Oh, I'm sure it's the right thing to do.' He smiled. 'I'll book the flight for the day after tomorrow—that'll give you time to get ready,' he said smoothly.

Helena looked up at him steadily. Why was he so certain she'd agree? She sniffed again. 'I'll make us some supper in a minute,' she said. She paused before turning to go upstairs. 'Oh, by the way, someone called earlier and left something for you,' she said.

Oscar glanced back, surprised. 'Oh? Who was it?'

Helena stared up at him, her face expressionless. 'It was a woman—she had two small boys with her. And she was very insistent that she spoke to you...that she and her sons...saw you, in person. She wouldn't tell me what it was all about.' Helena paused. 'The letter she left is on the kitchen table. I'm sure it will explain everything,' she added, treading firmly up the stairs.

CHAPTER NINE

For a long time after she'd gone upstairs, Helena sat staring out of the window at the familiar scene all around her, hating the thought of what it may look like if developers ever got their hands on Mulberry Court. She put her hand to her mouth as she imagined what it might become—a massive hotel…a huge commercial extension…and, worse, possibly a total demolition of the house, the entire property completely changed for ever. She shuddered as she imagined it.

And it was all very well for her to announce that *she* would never be party to selling to such people, she thought realistically, but even if a young family were to buy it—which Isobel had hoped might be the case—that didn't mean that eventually they, too, wouldn't sell to prospectors. Especially if the price was right. Helena knew that money was a powerful weapon, especially in the wrong hands. And the almost casual way in which Oscar had imparted the news convinced her that he didn't feel the same about the house as she did. He would look for the highest bidder, of course he would—he was a businessman. Well, he couldn't sell without *her* agreement, Helena thought decisively, and he was going to have to wait a long time for that!

She blew into Oscar's handkerchief again; she *was* getting a cold, she thought, wiping her eyes. But it wasn't just the cold that was irritating her tear ducts. She had several other reasons for feeling a bit low and, apart from the solicitor's news, they all concerned Oscar. Helena knew she was being unreasonable. So what if he did have numerous women in tow? Hardly a surprise and no more than she would have expected and, anyway, what did it matter to her? What if Allegra—whoever she was—had lost her baby?

And as for the woman and those children—they could be anybody...a family he'd known for ages, just trying to catch up before they went back home—wherever home was. In any case, none of this was any of her business, she told herself again angrily. She and Oscar were just old friends, nothing more, whose ways had parted a long time ago, and unexpectedly brought together again by the rather whimsical act of an elderly lady. And that time he'd kissed her, and any sensuous feelings which had happened between them in the past few weeks were totally unimportant...they didn't *mean* anything—to him. Oscar liked women—in every sense—and she, Helena, happened to be the woman he happened to be with at the moment. 'Allegra' or 'Callidora'—or anyone else—would have done just as well.

Telling herself this was all right up to a point, Helena started to slowly get ready for bed, but the unalterable and painful fact was that Oscar still had an intractable emotional hold over her, an unassailable ability to make her ecstatically happy, to revel in being anywhere near him and to admit again and again that she had never stopped loving him. Yet she had to accept the reality of their situation. This time next year Mulberry Court would no longer be theirs, she would be back in London with, presumably, enough money to buy herself a home of her own, and hopefully holding down a job which would keep her mind fully occupied, and away from pointless thoughts of the only man she had ever loved. And far, far away from imagining which woman he was spending his days with. His nights with...

All this introspection had made Helena temporarily forget Oscar's proclamation that they were going away for a short break. She sniffed. You could hardly call it a suggestion, she thought; he hadn't asked her whether she'd like to go or not—just that they were going, the day after tomorrow.

Helena had done very little travelling in her twenty-eight years, but had learned enough to whet the appetite. And it was after giving the matter a lot of thought she'd decided she would agree to go with Oscar, because it could be her only chance to see Greece—to see it with him. Something she'd once thought she might do one day. But this was not going to be a dream holiday, she assured herself—it was to be merely a mini-break, which busy people allowed themselves now and then. It would be a unique experience for her. And one which would never be repeated.

'We're going to a tiny island,' he'd informed her over supper. 'You'll love it. It's very beautiful but rather isolated, so you'll only need to pack a small amount of light stuff, and sensible footwear—and plenty of sun-block.'

On Saturday morning they arrived at the airport, and within twenty minutes they had been swiftly transported across the tarmac to Oscar's private jet. The speed with which it happened almost took Helena's breath away. The few times she'd flown anywhere, the waiting around to join various endless queues had been one of her abiding memories of airports. But today their arrangements were prompt and seamless and soon they were climbing the few steps into the aircraft. As she was shown into the cabin—which resembled a small, opulent sitting room—Helena wondered whether she was going to wake up in a minute. Was this really happening? she asked herself as she almost fell back into the luxurious depth of one of the armchairs.

Oscar sat down opposite her, stretching his arms above his head lazily. He was wearing dark trousers and a dark cotton shirt open at the neck, and he smiled lazily across at Helena, his perfect teeth blindingly white against the polished bronze of his tanned skin.

'I've ordered us some food once we are in the air,' he said briefly. 'Is that OK?'

Helena could only smile in response. She had nothing to complain about—so far! She knew she was excited—and she was going to put the sale of the house and her own future at the very back of her mind...just for these couple of days.

The one uniformed cabin attendant brought them their meal, served with iced water, and he spoke in rapid Greek to Oscar, who replied in the same way. As the steward backed away, it was quite obvious from the man's deferential attitude that Oscar was held in very high regard. Well, why wouldn't he be? It would be

Oscar's signature that appeared on the all-important pay cheques of his vast number of employees.

After the man had gone they began their meal, and Oscar leaned forward to fill their glasses with more water. And, presently, Helena put down her fork and sat back.

'I've never tasted stuffed vine leaves quite like those,' she murmured. 'Thank you, it was a very nice meal.'

Presently, their lunch things were removed and after a few minutes Oscar could see that Helena's eyelids were beginning to droop. 'How are you feeling?' he enquired briefly. She was looking pale, and winsomely desirable, dressed in a long rust-coloured cotton skirt and a soft cream top which exposed her slender neck and shoulders.

'Much better,' Helena said, sitting forward at once, but he gestured for her to relax.

'Have a sleep for an hour or so,' he said easily. 'When we land, there'll be a car to take us to the quay. And a private ferry will get us to the island. And then I'll show you one of the best places in the whole world.'

By mid-afternoon they were aboard the small private ferry which would take them to their destination. Aristi, the boat owner, greeted Oscar very enthusiastically, shaking him by the hand as he welcomed them on board, and casting a dark, appreciative glance in Helena's direction.

It was a very hot day and Oscar looked down at Helena as they stood together at the prow of the small vessel, letting the cool draught fan their faces. 'Aristi informs me that this weather is going to continue for some weeks,' he said. 'It's a shame we only have a couple of days, but that'll be long enough for me to show you around.' He pushed his sunglasses on to the top of his head for a moment. 'On the whole, it's quite a barren landscape, with just enough fertile land to support a small area of olive trees and vines, but it's not a popular place with tourists because there's very little on offer other than the natural beauty and solitude of the place. And the local population is small,' he added.

'So, what do people do with themselves?' Helena wanted to know.

'Oh, they keep goats, and work the land where they can—and there's a small harbour which provides a useful living for some,' Oscar replied. 'He looked down at her. 'Civilization roughly comprises a small hamlet of about a dozen houses—there are a couple of bars, and a taverna—which is where I always stay. The locals go over to the mainland for their other various needs,' he added.

Helena looked at him pensively. In spite of all the places that someone as wealthy as Oscar could go to recharge his batteries from time to time, the remote island she was about to see was where he liked best. And of course it was close enough to Athens—and work—for him to get back easily enough. It warmed her heart to think that this rich, vastly important man enjoyed the simple pleasures of life.

They arrived at a small jetty and Aristi helped them off the boat, shaking Oscar's hand vigorously before setting off again back to the mainland, shouting, *'Ade ha'sou! Kali tihi!'* as he went.

Oscar glanced down at Helena. 'He was hoping we'd have a nice day—and wishing us good luck,' he explained and he smiled inwardly. He was fairly certain he wasn't going to need any luck.

Oscar was carrying their two holdalls and they started walking up and away from the jetty, Helena wearing her large sun hat.

'The taverna is only about a mile away,' he said, glancing down at Helena's feet. 'Are you OK to walk in those sandals?'

'Perfectly, thanks,' she said, though thinking that maybe she should have worn her deck shoes. The ground was dusty and rather stony, and after only a few minutes some tiny bits of gravel began filtering in between her toes. But she'd grit her teeth, she thought. She wasn't going to complain this early on in their 'holiday'.

The picture Oscar had painted of the island had led Helena to think that it was far more remote than it turned out to be, because within twenty minutes they came to a small cluster of white-painted, cube-shaped houses, whose blue-shuttered windows were partly obscured by pots of flame-red geraniums, suggesting a kind of carnival atmosphere. In almost every small patch of garden were one or two tethered goats. And all around them were flourishing bushes of bougainvillea, and the tangible, overpowering perfume of rosemary and other sweet-scented herbs.

'This is "civilization",' Oscar said briefly.

'*Oh,*' Helena breathed. 'What a *pretty* scene; it's like a picture book!'

Oscar looked down at her, pleased at her reaction.

Helena smiled up at him, knowing that she was going to love being here, despite the intense heat, which she could only tolerate for so long. 'It's very quiet,' she said, lowering her voice so as not to disturb the pervading silence, and Oscar nodded.

'It's still siesta time,' he said. 'Everyone sleeps during the afternoon, but I know Alekos will be about, because he's expecting us.' He darted a quick glance at Helena. 'Are you OK to keep walking? We'll be there in just a few minutes.'

'I'm fine,' Helena replied.

Presently, they came to the taverna, which, Helena could see, was a somewhat larger version of the other houses on the island, but with an open frontage sporting decking on which were two small tables and wooden chairs shaded by blue-striped canopies which moved gently in the rather sparse breeze. There were balconies all around the first floor, bedecked with showers of more red geraniums, and under the shade of an adjacent olive tree a silent donkey stood, its head bowed, and it didn't even look up as the two approached.

'Alekos has had that ancient animal for years,' Oscar said. 'I don't think it does much carrying any more—trucks are used now, of course. But in the old days, donkeys did all the work.'

Oscar ushered Helena in before him, and she breathed a small sigh of relief to be in the shade of the building. Hearing their footsteps, a small, excitable, black-eyed, black-haired middle-aged man came forward, uttering, to Helena, unintelligible words of welcome as he embraced Oscar, banging him furiously on the back, his deeply olive complexion creased in genuine smiles of delight.

'*Oscarrr!*' the man exclaimed. '*Ya su! Pos ise?*'

'I'm good, thanks, Alekos,' Oscar said, releasing the man's affectionate hold, and looking down at Helena. 'This is Helena, Alekos, and she does not speak our language…'

The man immediately took Helena's hand and kissed it effusively. 'Of course…I am sorry! We shall continue in English! Come…come…drinks, water…?'

They all went into the sitting room and Helena took off her hat and ran her fingers through her dampened hair. What she'd like now, she thought, was a long, cool shower.

'Where is Adrienne?' Oscar asked Alekos, and the older man grinned.

'My wife is in Athens! With our daughter! Because we have a new grandson, Petros—God be praised!' Alekos exclaimed. 'Adrienne will be returning in three days—but you are going before then?' the older man asked.

'Afraid so,' Oscar said. 'But many, many congratulations, Alekos! A child! What a blessing!' he exclaimed.

'*Neh!*' Alekos agreed. 'And a boy! God be praised!' he repeated.

After other pleasantries had been exchanged and the three had sat in the darkened interior refreshing themselves with their drinks, Alekos led them up the stairs to a sparsely furnished room in which there was a massive bed spread with a pure white cover, a thick bolster and pillows at the head. The floors were wooden, with no carpeting of any kind, there were two small cabinets with drawers, and two chairs. The shutters at the windows were tightly shut to keep out the heat, giving the room a cool, secretive atmosphere. And to the side was a minute room with shower and toilet.

After Alekos had departed, Helena sat gingerly on the edge of the bed and looked up at Oscar. She realized that she hadn't given any thought to where they might be staying—she'd just followed Oscar's plans, with no questions asked. But now she realized she was feeling stupidly shy at the position she was in... They were going to be sharing a bed. How was she going to deal with that? she asked herself, feeling frantic at the thought. Although they had been close, very close, a long time ago, they had never actually slept together, not in the accepted sense of that phrase. And things were different now; he had moved on—and away. She swallowed hard as their eyes met.

Then, as if reading her thoughts, Oscar said, 'Europeans go in for wide beds,' he said casually. 'Useful—and necessary—in hot climates.'

And, with that, he kicked off his shoes and flopped down on the other side of the bed, well away from Helena. He yawned, not looking at her. 'After we've had a rest and a shower, I'll take you exploring. Alekos will be making us one of his superb suppers. Which we won't be eating until much later in the evening when everything's cooled down.'

Oscar closed his eyes, waiting for Helena to say something, but instead he heard her take off her sandals and lie down quietly beside him, positioning herself almost on the edge of her side of the bed. He smiled inwardly. He'd waited this long; he could wait a bit longer, he thought… Wait for that special moment…

It was seven o'clock before they both surfaced, Oscar first, and for several minutes he lay on his side, propped up on his elbow, just drinking in Helena's appearance. Her skirt was pulled up around her thighs and her loose top had fallen slightly, exposing the rounded curve of her breasts in the lacy bra. She'd pulled the clip from her hair, which hung loosely around her shoulders, and her face was pale in sleep—pale and perfect, he thought, longing to touch her. He shifted slightly, and the movement made Helena wake with a start. She sat up quickly, drawing her skirt down and looking across at him.

'How long have we been asleep?' she asked. 'I can't believe I dropped off so easily!'

'That's what the Greek climate does to you,' Oscar said, getting up and swinging his legs off the bed. He glanced back. 'I'll have a shower first, allow you to wake up properly. Then I'll show you around my is-land. It'll be getting cool now.'

Later, both having changed into light shorts and fresh tops—and with Helena wearing her deck shoes, they set off.

'You can walk the whole island in a couple of hours or so,' Oscar said briefly. 'But tonight we'll head down to the little cove I like best. It's usually nice and breezy down there.'

As they made their way across the rough ground together, Helena took a deep breath. Not just because of where they were, and of the tangible sense of peace and tranquillity, but because she and Oscar were alone, just the two of them again, just strolling along as they used to do, talking only when they felt like it, absorbing their togetherness. Helena was not going to think of anything else, not allow her anxieties about her life to spoil these precious moments which would never come again. At this point in time her heart felt like a singing bird.

Just then, her foot caught on something and she staggered slightly, lurching forward. But not before Oscar had caught her, holding her to him briefly.

'Careful,' he murmured. Then, 'It gets easier in a minute.' But he didn't let go of her, clasping her hand in his tightly as they walked on, with Oscar pointing out certain things that interested him.

As they started to make their way down towards the sea, they came across a tiny white-washed domed chapel, and Helena glanced up at Oscar.

'Could we go inside…just for a second?' she asked, thinking that she would like to say one or two things to her guardian angel.

Oscar made no comment, but led the way towards the door, which was partially open. As they went inside, Helena almost choked with emotion as she looked around. The place was cool, dark, mysterious, with just three small rows of chairs leading to an altar on which was a single tall candle, a simple cross and a gilded icon. And below was a small prayer table on which were a few lit candles flickering softly.

After she'd taken in her surroundings, Helena went forward slowly and stood gazing up for a moment. Then, turning to Oscar who had come up behind her, she said softly, 'Did you bring any money with you? I would like to…I would like to light a candle…'

Immediately, Oscar withdrew a note from his pocket, slipping it into the donation box, and Helena lit a candle and placed it alongside the others. Then she moved over to the nearest chair and knelt down, closing her eyes. She knew she'd have to stay there for a moment until she'd regained her composure because the whole atmosphere was making tears well up behind her eyelids, and she did not want to make a fool of herself in front of Oscar, who she didn't imagine had her spiritual sensitivity.

But Oscar had moved right away from her, allowing her privacy, and when she got up and turned back to him he reached out his hand and took hers again, not saying anything. He led her back out into the softly darkening night and she looked up at him gratefully.

'Thanks,' she said. 'At that moment, I had an overwhelming need to ask for something.'

He smiled down at her, releasing her hand and putting his arm around her shoulders instead. 'What were you asking for? Or am I not allowed to ask?' he said.

'Well, seeing that you paid for my candle, you are entitled to know that,' Helena said, feeling so utterly, utterly happy and contented she could tell him anything.

'I was asking that Mulberry Court is always looked after properly, and that it never gets into the hands of the wrong people, that it will never become a monstrous, money-making place that would have horrified Isobel,' she said slowly. 'And that whoever eventually owns the house…and the wonderful land surrounding it...will give it the love and cherishing that it's always been used to.'

Oscar made no comment, yet Helena was somehow aware that he understood her feelings; the occasional pressure of his hand on her bare shoulder as he tucked her in closer said things that needed no words...not just then.

By the time they got to the little beach, the light was finally beginning to fade. They found a small sandy hillock and Oscar sat first, pulling Helena down beside him, and as they looked up into the night sky the visible universe appeared before them, a myriad tiny stars twinkling in their thousands, as if thrown there carelessly by an overindulgent god.

Sitting up, with her arms wrapped around her knees, Helena said, 'Even in this light, the sea still looks a beautiful colour, doesn't it...I noticed it when we were coming across this afternoon—shades of azure and turquoise and emerald, all mixed up.' She glanced down at Oscar, who'd been gazing up at her. 'I can't say I've ever noticed colours in the water like that anywhere else before.'

He smiled at her, his dark-fringed eyes gleaming in the dusk. 'We have our very own god Apollo to thank for that,' he murmured. 'He continues to send us a permanent supply of an extra-special light to produce such fluorescence.' Oscar paused. 'I'm glad you noticed,' he added.

Looking away, Helena put her head on one side thoughtfully. Was he teasing her because of what she'd said in the chapel? Did he really give any credence to the idea of other-worldly beings? Perhaps he, too, had a guardian angel, some unseen presence that he needed to get in touch with now and then. She smiled inwardly. That the all-important, almost obscenely successful Oscar Theotokis might need anything, or anyone, other than his own self-belief, was a most unlikely thought.

They sat there for several minutes, basking in the warmth of the night. Then Oscar's meltingly sexy tone interrupted Helena's dreamy thinking.

'*Heleena,*' he murmured quietly.

Drawing her down to lie beside him on the soft sand, he turned towards her on his side, lowering his head to close his mouth over hers, and Helena, her heart leaping in response to his touch, knew that she was lost, utterly lost. She was here in this divine place with the most desirable man in the world, and nothing, ever again, was going to compare with this brief interlude in her life.

She closed her eyes, loving the feel of his lips parting hers, the gentle thrust of his tongue, the feel of his hands entwining her hair as he bent over her. She kissed him back with increasing fervour, lost in the urgency of her need, not caring that these were to be temporary, passing moments that would never come again...

'*Heleena,*' he said again softly, gazing down into her now wide eyes. Then he began undressing her, touching each part of her with his lips as he went, her pale forehead, the tip of her nose, the tender skin at the base of her throat, the round smoothness of her naked body, knowing that he was heightening her unashamed passion, bringing it to the stratospheric level of his own...

'You make me so happy, *Heleena,*' he murmured,

gazing down at her. 'You always, always made me so happy...'

And all Helena could do was to whisper his name, over and over again. *'Oscar...Oscar...'* He was so gorgeous, she thought, feeling almost dazed in ecstasy at the feel of him, at the sight of him, his dark, suntanned skin shining faintly with perspiration, his hair glistening black in the soft light. *My Oscar...*

Gently, tenderly, he went on making slow, passionate love to her, knowing that neither of them wanted it to end quickly. As she felt his vigorous, naked body against hers Helena felt shafts of indescribable pleasure ripple through her and she moved restlessly beneath him, clinging to him with increasing intensity, her breathlessness becoming painful, and she kept on whispering his name again and again...

And then, finally, he was inside her, and their worlds exploded in a dramatic firework display of wave upon wave of heated emotion until exhausted, sated, they lay back side by side, holding hands, saying nothing to disturb their sublime contentment.

And they remained there, silent as statues, until they saw Venus sink slowly in the west.

CHAPTER TEN

LATER, with their arms around each other's waists, they strolled back to the taverna, neither of them wanting to spoil their ecstatic moment on the beach by soiling the memory with words.

Helena glanced up at Oscar, admiring for the millionth time the chiselled contours of his face, the broad forehead, the firm mouth which had claimed hers with such intensity that she could still feel her lips tingling.

'Alekos seemed very happy at having a grandson,' she said presently.

'Well, of course he is,' Oscar said. 'Families are an essential part of the Greek culture, and having a boy child is considered extremely fortunate. For obvious reasons,' he added dryly.

He said no more, and Helena shot him a look, realizing that Oscar's own family must be very thankful that he was there to shoulder the burden of their company. But after him...then who? she thought.

Their rather late meal of thinly sliced boiled octopus in olive oil on a bed of glistrada leaves wouldn't have been Helena's first choice, but she was surprised at how much she enjoyed it. Alekos was clearly very experienced at presenting tasty dishes for his visitors, and the man's delight when he collected their empty plates was palpable.

Presently, after sharing more than one bottle of local wine with Alekos to christen the new baby's head, Helena and Oscar made their way upstairs. And when Helena cast her eyes once more on that snowy-white bed, she had no sense of trepidation, only a warm rush of pleasure at the thought of lying there with Oscar. Of being close. Of feeling his warmth meld with hers.

And in the small hours of the morning, he came to her again, embracing her tenderly, inviting her to make another journey of love within his arms. And this time it was even more wonderful than before because now they knew each other, and the familiarity of the moments only enhanced the sensual act taking place.

Then, finally, cradled in each other's arms, the surging tides of passion gave way to blissful, wonderful peace, and at last the lovers slept.

The rest of their break passed in a blur to Helena, and soon they were once more flying back towards London.

Sitting opposite her in the aircraft, Oscar gazed across at Helena, wondering what was going through her mind, what lay behind the expression in those beautiful, sometimes sad and soulful eyes.

The few days had passed exactly as he'd planned—and he knew that Helena had enjoyed it. Had enjoyed *them*. But that still didn't tell him what he really wanted to know, where exactly their paths might lead, how exactly this last chapter was going to be written. He shifted in his seat and leaned forward to stare out of the window.

And, for herself, Helena was feeling more than slightly confused at her present situation with Oscar. Their short holiday had been beyond wonderful, she thought. Their lovemaking had been fantastic, unbelievable and had sent her into paroxysms of joy she would never be able to easily describe.

And yet, and yet…Oscar had not told her he loved her. The three words she wanted to hear him say, the three words that every woman needed to hear. She knew that he'd wanted her—in the erotic sense. Oh yes, he'd made that plain enough. As much as she had wanted him. But all he had murmured over and over again was that she made him happy…that was all. She—made—him—happy. Was that enough? And what did it really mean? Did he imply that *they* could be happy again together? Or was it that their mutual pleasure had given him just a passing happiness?

She frowned as her thoughts tormented her. Was it merely the sort of happiness that went with satisfied lust? Something which he could obtain quite easily with others? And doubtless very frequently did? Or was it more significant? She bit her lip. She would probably never know the answers to all that, she thought.

They had both been rather quiet that morning, perhaps not relishing the thought of picking up the strands of normal life again. Helena looked across at Oscar, noting the familiar determined set of his jaw. His mind was probably already fixated on the work which would be waiting for him when they returned to Mulberry Court, she thought. Their holiday romance was at an end—and wasn't that to be expected? All holiday flings came to nothing, everyone knew that. They were merely passing flights of temporal fantasy. So?…So? Well, just live with it, she told herself.

She wished—not for the first time—that she could spend a few hours with her friend Anna and pour out her heart. Anna was one of those people who seemed able to read the lives and problems of others and come up with definitive answers—or, at any rate, some sound advice. But although the two girls had had several conversations on the phone since Helena had come to Dorset, Helena could never bring herself to talk about Oscar—had deliberately been evasive when questioned about the other person involved in the will. And, anyway, although Anna and Helena had been close over the years, Helena had never revealed details of her youthful love affair to another living soul because it would have been too painful. And pointless. Pointless going over something which had ended, and which it would have been far better never to have begun.

Much later, Oscar and Helena arrived back at Mulberry Court and, having eaten during their journey, no more food was considered necessary. All Helena wanted to do was to shower and get some sleep. With her foot on the bottom stair, she looked back at Oscar, who'd said he would be doing work in the study before going to bed himself.

'Goodnight, Oscar,' she said to his departing back. 'And…um…thank you…thank you for my…holiday.' She paused. 'I loved your island,' she added softly.

He turned briefly and gazed up at her, his heart almost bursting with love for her, his fertile mind doing somersaults, longing to tell her, longing to know…

'I knew you would like it there as much as I do,' he

said. And then, impulsively, he added, 'By the way, I want you to know…um…I don't want you to lose any sleep about the future of Mulberry Court.'

Helena stared back at him. 'I'll try not to…' she began, and he interrupted.

'No, what I mean is that I'm not going to sell this place—to strangers, I mean.' He cleared his throat. 'I intend keeping it, keeping it in the Theotokis family, where it belongs. And I intend…I shall be bringing my wife here one day—if I can persuade her to see my point of view,' he added obliquely.

Frozen to the spot as she stared up at him, Helena felt as if she was going to pass out. His *wife*? What wife? she asked herself incredulously. He'd never mentioned a wife before, and in fact he'd implied that he would probably never marry anyone! She forced herself to appear unperturbed by what he'd just said.

'Oh, well…' she swallowed '…it's a great relief that you intend saving Mulberry Court from a terrible fate.' She paused. 'I hope your wife will appreciate the place as much as we…as much as I…have always done,' she added.

Oscar gazed down, his eyes gleaming blackly. 'Oh, I know her well enough to be absolutely certain that she will,' he said slowly. 'And I know she'll love living here for as much of the year as is possible, allowing for work commitments. She'll have to understand that we'll need to be away fairly regularly,' he added.

'Oh, I'm sure she'll fall in with all your requirements, Oscar,' Helena said tightly.

He shrugged. 'I hope so,' he said, 'but women can be…unpredictable…at times.'

Helena could think of several ways to respond to that remark, but thought better of it. Instead, she turned and went resolutely up the stairs.

''Night,' she said casually over her shoulder, before going into her room and shutting the door firmly.

For a full five minutes she stood there, her blood racing through her veins. If Oscar had taken a gun and shot her through the heart, she couldn't feel more shocked and empty. How could he even *mention* a wife to her after what had taken place between them under the stars only a few days ago? What *was* it with men, that they could switch passion on and off like that? And what was it with Oscar Theotokis that he could treat women like he did…and that they came back for more? As she had done! Perhaps if—and when—he introduced them, she should tell Oscar's lady love just what she'd be taking on!

Helena sat down on her bed with a thump. One thing was certain—no Greek woman was going to like being in England for very long, she thought fiercely; they wouldn't survive the variable temperatures of the local climate. There wasn't usually any need to slap on the factor five thousand *here*! And, whoever she was, she'd soon start complaining when it rained for two weeks without stopping!

Then Helena's shoulders drooped. Who else would appreciate this very special place as she did? she asked herself. Who else would know the warm, personal welcome that filled every room in the house, who else would ever bother to roam every corner of the grounds, find out where the wild flowers peeped out in early spring, or want to help with fruit picking in the autumn? Or want to take a book and have a lazy read inside the long, sheltering branches of the willow tree? It would be a complete waste to bring another woman here, she thought, especially one not used to the simple pleasures in life. She would just not fit in. And she'd make Oscar's life a misery, always wanting to get back where the sun perpetually shone.

As she started to unpack her holdall listlessly, Helena knew that none of that mattered. This was all about Oscar. Nothing to do with the ownership of a property. And the unpalatable truth was that she was jealous—jealous as hell to think of anyone else being his wife even though he'd never given her any reason to think he'd want her, Helena, to fill that role. He'd never told her that, or even hinted at it. Oscar didn't want her, had never wanted her—not in a lasting, bonding sense.

She gripped her hands together tightly. Oh, why, why, *why* had Isobel thrown them together again? she asked herself desperately.

And downstairs Oscar admitted to feeling bad, feeling uncomfortable at what he'd said to Helena. It had been disingenuous, to put it mildly, but at the last second something had made him hesitate before going on to say what was really in his mind and heart.

His jaw tightened. With their past history, he knew he was standing on uneven emotional ground with Helena—and he had to be careful not to take a false step. He knew that she desired him, but could she risk trusting him? Would she ever take another chance with him, and was it fair of him to expect it? His eyes nar-

rowed. All was fair in love and war, and he'd do whatever it took to convince her. And wait for that golden
moment when he would make it impossible for Helena
to refuse him.

Next day, Helena woke up feeling surprisingly in charge
of her emotions. Even though Oscar's mind-boggling
announcement last night had taken the wind right out of
her sails, at least he would see that no wretched development took place here, she thought. Mulberry Court
was going to be safe. And, anyway, he'd wanted to buy
her out all along, so he'd be getting his wish. No sur-
prises there. Oscar was used to getting his own way.
He had the powerful personality—and the money—
to do it.

And she should also be grateful that he'd left her in
no doubt that when choosing a wife he wasn't looking
in her direction! Because any man who could transport
a woman to such dizzy heights of emotion—and then
act as if it had meant nothing—wasn't worth the time of
day! Not in *her* book! Oscar didn't know the meaning
of true love—unconditional, selfless love. Passion—
of course—naturally! But love, true love, which meant
permanent bonding? Forget it!

Helena marched over to the chest of drawers for
some fresh clothes. Whoever Oscar's future unknown
wife was out there, she thought…well, she had *her* sympathy!

It was gone nine o'clock before Helena went down
into the kitchen to make herself some breakfast. As
she passed the study, she could hear Oscar. He was obviously speaking on the telephone and his voice was

raised, sounding urgent. Helena made a face to herself. It had been amazing that he'd managed to actually have almost three days away without someone contacting him, she thought.

She put the kettle on to make some tea and took bread from the freezer to make toast. Oscar could join her when it suited him, she thought, laying two places at the table and putting grounds into the cafetière for his coffee, forcing herself to hum a little tune. She'd made up her mind to act perfectly normally when she came face to face with him today, as if she hadn't given another thought to what he'd said last night. And, after all, what had changed? Nothing, she told herself. She was back to square one, having a simple break away from London for a few weeks, except that there was nothing simple about it. It would have been if Oscar wasn't part of the equation…if they'd never met up again, if he hadn't whisked her off to that sunlit island…

Suddenly, her mobile rang. It was Anna, and hearing her friend's voice made Helena's heart lift instantly. After the two girls had exchanged greetings, Anna said, 'You remember that position I told you about here… the vacancy I knew was coming up? Well, it has— much sooner than I'd thought—they want it filled by the beginning of August, and they're going to be interviewing shortly, but you'll have to get your application in on time.' Anna stopped for breath before going on, 'This sort of opportunity doesn't often come up in our place, so I hope you'll go for it, Helena—it's just your thing, I know it is! And you'd fit in a treat! And wouldn't it be fantastic to be seeing more of each other again? I miss you, Helena! It seems ages since we had some fun together. I'll send all the details to Mulberry Court tonight, shall I, and then you can think it over. OK? But don't leave it late, will you…?' And, as an afterthought, 'You must be feeling right back to your old self by now, lapping up all that peace and quiet, not to mention being totally free from the deadly male species for a change!' It had been Anna who had helped mop up Helena's tears after the failed relationship with Mark. 'And don't forget, you can always stay with us until you find your dream home!' Anna said cheerfully.

Helena smiled broadly. It was so good to hear her friend's voice, especially this morning.

The two girls spent a few minutes while Anna filled in more details about the job and just catching up, then they finished the call and Helena snapped her mobile shut thoughtfully. That was just what she needed. Not just to hear Anna's voice, but to make her realize that she should think seriously about her future. It was time to turn her back on Mulberry Court and return to real life. Being here, she was hiding her head in the sand.

She was just making her tea when Oscar appeared, and she glanced up. 'Hi,' she said brightly. 'Do you want your coffee now?'

He came across and stood next to her and Helena thought, please don't touch me. I don't want you to ever touch me again. She took a step to the side, avoiding any contact, and took their drinks over to the table.

'I've just had a very interesting call from Anna—my friend in London,' she said, glancing up at him briefly. 'She told me about a very exciting opportunity coming up in her firm. She's going to send me all the details so that I can apply.' Helena sat down and reached for the rack of toast. 'It does sound as if it might suit me,' she went on, spreading some butter on her slice of toast, 'and if I was lucky enough to get it, I wouldn't start until August so I'd still have a few weeks here. So that would be good, wouldn't it?' She took a generous bite from the toast and scrunched away, looking up at him, realizing that he hadn't spoken a word.

'I have to go back to Greece as soon as possible, now, this morning,' he said, his expression darkly serious.

'Well, I hope you can stop long enough to have your coffee,' Helena said, rather tritely.

He stared down at her. 'I've just been told they've brought my father back to Greece,' he said quietly. 'I'm afraid he's dying.'

CHAPTER ELEVEN

A WEEK later Louise returned and Helena was especially thankful to have some company. To hear about someone else's problems was always a relief, she thought, as one morning she made her way down to the cottages.

Oscar had left almost immediately after receiving the call from Greece, only staying long enough to have a quick coffee, refusing any food. It was obvious that the news had hit him unbelievably hard, and Helena was filled with sympathy as she'd looked up at his drawn features. She was never going to forget what her reaction had been on hearing about her own father's death, how she'd felt so devastated, so empty. She knew that losing one's parents was a natural sequence of human events, but that didn't make it any more acceptable when it happened.

She had found it easy to offer just one or two words of sympathy, squeezing Oscar's arm tightly, and he'd covered her hand with his own briefly. With his voice thick with worry, he'd said he would be in touch with her as soon as possible. And, rather surprisingly, given the particular circumstances, as he'd left he had asked her not to apply for the London job until he returned, saying it could complicate matters. And although

Helena hadn't really understood the point, she wasn't going to question it…not then. Family matters were a far more important concern than jobs—or even the selling of houses. And that was obviously the 'complication' he was alluding to, she thought. His buying Mulberry Court from her and all the formalities that would have to be dealt with. And he knew that, now, she would readily fall in with his plan because it meant no one else would get their grasping hands on the place.

All the information about the job had arrived in the post two days later and, leafing through it, Helena had to agree with Anna that it did seem to fit her credentials perfectly, almost tailor-made for her, in fact. But there was no need to return the forms just yet, she'd thought, putting them back into the envelope. Not until she'd spoken to Oscar. She'd had only one rather tense call from him, telling her very little, and she remembered what he'd said about Greeks being very family-oriented and emotionally close. His parents were Oscar's only family, as far as she knew, and it was his father's name which had always cropped up in conversations. In a way, Helena wished she was there with him to give some support, but he'd have no need of her. There'd be plenty of other people—other women—to give him support. Not to mention his future wife!

Now, Helena tapped lightly on the door of Louise's cottage and Benjamin, with Rosie at his heels and a mug of coffee in his hand, opened it to let Helena come in. Louise came across from the kitchen with some drinks on a tray, her face creased in a broad smile.

'It's so good to be home again,' she said, putting down the tray and giving Helena a big hug. 'Now, I know we've only had a few words on the phone so far, but I want to know everything that's been happening!' She handed Helena a mug of coffee.

Helena said quickly, 'You start first, Louise—how's your cousin now?'

Benjamin cleared his throat, looking at each of them in turn. 'Well, Rosie and I must be off—so I'll leave you two to it,' he said amiably. He glanced across at Louise. 'Thanks for the coffee, Louise—the best one I've had for weeks!'

'Flatterer,' Louise said as she handed Helena a plate of biscuits. 'And by the way, I'm making a steak and kidney pudding for supper, Benjamin. I know it's your favourite, so we'll eat at eight, if that's OK.' She looked across at Helena. 'There'll be plenty for three if you'd like to join us, Helena,' she said, adding, 'It's wonderful to be using my own cooker again. Didn't realize how much I'd miss it!'

After Benjamin had gone, and Helena had insisted on knowing every detail about Sarah's problems, Louise said, 'Now, I want to know how *you've* been getting on.' She shot a look at Helena. 'Benjamin told me that Oscar's been about quite a lot…'

'Yes…he has been, on and off,' Helena replied guardedly. She smiled. 'I think he wants to keep a very close eye on his property, but at the moment he's with his father, who's not at all well, I understand,' she added, deciding not to be more specific.

'Mmm,' Louise murmured equivocally. She paused, then, casually, 'Benjamin and I were chatting the other night, and we came up with the idea that wouldn't it be wonderful if you and Mr Oscar were to, you know, keep the house and…were to get married one day…'

Helena interrupted this flight of fancy. 'Louise! There's about as much chance of that happening as time moving backwards!' she exclaimed. 'Oscar would never want to marry me, I know that for a fact.'

'I don't see why not,' Louise said. 'It's obvious that he…likes you…Helena. Always did. Just think of the hours you both spent here together…'

She didn't go on, but Louise remembered those times clearly—what a handsome couple the youthful pair had made, how they'd revelled in each other's company… and it was no different now, not from the looks she'd seen Oscar give Helena…

Helena shrugged. 'We've both grown up, Louise,' she said firmly. 'And anyway, if Oscar ever marries, it won't be to an Englishwoman. He'll probably have to marry a suitable Greek woman.'

Louise pursed her lips. 'Well, Isobel's husband obviously had his own ideas about that,' she said. 'Now, those two were a devoted couple. He worshipped the ground Isobel walked on.'

'They were a different generation, Louise, and Oscar is obviously different from Paul Theotokis,' Helena said lightly, not wishing to continue with this conversation. She wasn't going to say a word about the wife Oscar had alluded to, nor that he intended becoming the sole owner of Mulberry Court. In any case, that was still some time off because no sale could go through until one year had elapsed—which was still some time away. Best to leave things unsaid, for now, she thought. But she couldn't help feeling touched at what Louise obviously hoped for, though Helena hadn't realized that she and Oscar had obviously been discussed at length by the two in the cottages. And of course their dream scenario would be wonderful for them, she thought. The perfect answer to their own personal future.

For the next few days, Helena decided to suspend all thoughts about Oscar, or the house, or the London job, until he came back to England. She still had another couple of weeks before the application form needed to be sent, so she decided to spend a lot of the time being busy cataloguing all the books in the library, even though she knew this wasn't really her problem any more. She made notes of the ones she would like to take away for herself, thinking that it would be useful for Oscar to know exactly what was left on those shelves. Kneeling back on her heels, she added another set of volumes to the list in her hand. And the moisture she was wiping from her eyes had little to do with the occasional dust that drifted about, she knew that. It was sad regret that made her keep taking a tissue from her pocket.

One day, Helena went upstairs to her room, taking her mug of tea with her. She put it on the bedside table, then sat looking around her again for a moment. All the rooms in Mulberry Court were individually distinguished by the furniture and fittings that Isobel had brought back from her travels, and Helena's room— the best one, in her opinion—boasted several items of beautiful hand-crafted Indian workmanship. She stared thoughtfully at her reflection in the ornate mirror opposite, and at its matching chest of drawers. Both items had apparently been the handiwork of a young teenager—the son of the owner of a struggling out-of-town enterprise in Delhi—and, staring at it now, Helena knew that she wanted this special furniture in her own home one day. Well, it wouldn't suit Oscar's style, she thought. He wouldn't want it.

Suddenly, remembering something, Helena smiled faintly and stood up and went over to kneel in front of the chest of drawers. Apart from the one in which she'd put some clean tops, they were empty of any contents but, at Helena's touch, the wider drawer at the bottom slid open smoothly. She let her fingers trace the fine inside seam along its length until she felt the tiny nub which, when compressed, allowed the opening of a compartment designed as a place of safety for treasures.

'I thought it was such fun!' Isobel had said when she'd first shown it to Helena. 'Such amazing crafts-manship by someone so young, with a delightfully cunning twist! I had never seen anything like it before, and I think everyone should have somewhere special that no one else knows about! And this is yours, this is for you, Helena,' she'd declared emphatically.

Now, with the firm movement required, Helena was able to draw out the small compartment and, gasping audibly, she felt her fingers close on something inside. Bending further forward, she took out two envelopes and stared at them for a moment, completely mystified.

With her mouth drying, she recognized the first one immediately. It was something she had found in her father's desk after he had died and, without question, Helena had obeyed the simple hand-written instruction on the front.

'To be returned, unopened, to Mrs Isobel Theotokis.'

Now, with the blood beginning to gather pace through her arteries, Helena picked up the second envelope. It read:

'For the sole attention of Miss Helena Kingston.'

Holding both items in her hands, which were by now shaking, Helena wondered if she was having another of her dreams, whether she was finally losing her grip on reality. She stayed quite still for several minutes, then got up slowly and went over to sit down on the cushioned seat under the window.

Then she opened each envelope carefully and spread the contents out in front of her.

Finally, the worst had happened and, ten days later, Oscar was due to return to Mulberry Court. Helena's feelings were in a state of total confusion as she waited to see his car pull up outside.

From their one or two phone conversations, Helena had learned that Giorgios Theotokis had passed away quietly with Oscar there, holding his hand. From the tone of his voice, and the brevity of what he'd said, Helena knew that it had—naturally—been a traumatic event for Oscar. But she also knew that he would deal with it—and the aftermath—quickly and effectively, in his usual businesslike way. He was no defeatist, and he would recover, probably quicker than she had done after her own bereavement.

But, in spite of death, life went on, Helena reminded herself. And *her* life was somewhat hanging in the balance. She still had no job, and no home of her own that she could move into. In fact, the only thing that she really owned at the moment was an elderly car waiting to be picked up at that London garage.

And that other thing she owned. A broken, jealous heart…

Then a sudden smile tilted the corners of her mouth. Despite everything else, she had to acknowledge a warm ripple of contentment running through her every now and again. It was possible, she realized, to feel happiness—real happiness—on someone else's behalf, even in retrospect. Happiness by proxy! Even the darkest clouds sometimes had a silver lining, she thought.

At six o'clock on the Friday evening that Oscar was due back, Helena stood idly in the conservatory, gazing out of the window. He had phoned her on his way from the airport to say that there was heavy traffic and that he might be delayed.

She had been surprised that he was able to return to the UK so soon after the funeral—she'd have thought there'd have still been a great deal to do. But when she'd made the comment to Oscar, he'd said that there were one or two essential points he had to clarify regarding Mulberry Court, and that he wanted to get them sorted out as quickly as possible.

In the fridge were some thick, moist slices of home-cooked gammon, and a generous wedge of duck paté to go with a loaf of the bread she'd bought for their supper, and presently she went into the kitchen to prepare a green salad to go with it all. In the new car—which Helena freely admitted she was going to hate parting with—she'd driven into Dorchester that morning to buy the provisions—among which were some delicious black cherries, which now she rinsed under the tap before putting them in a ceramic bowl.

It had been a lovely fine day, and the evening was turning out to be just as perfect, with the sun still warm and a light breeze ruffling the leaves and branches. Glancing at her watch for the hundredth time, Helena decided that she wasn't going to waste another moment inside; her days here were numbered, and it could be another hour or more before Oscar returned.

She tore a piece of paper from the notepad in her bag and scribbled the words '6.45—gone for a short walk'. Then she propped it up against one of the wine glasses on the table and went outside.

She was wearing her simple blue shift dress and strappy sandals, her hair in one long plait down her back and, as soon as she set off, Helena's heart surged once more in pleasure just to be here, walking the familiar territory. As she trod lightly across the dry grass, her mind kept going back to the short time on that island... Well, it had been in the forefront of her thoughts ever since they'd returned. How could it not have been? It had been an unforgettable few days and she never would, never could, forget it. How could Oscar have brought her down to earth so cruelly—on the very night they'd come back? It had been heartless of him to even hint at another woman after he'd possessed her so fully! Even if he did know that announcing he was going to keep Mulberry Court in the family would please her! As if that made everything all right! Her heart, and this house, were two very different things, she thought, suddenly feeling defiant again at what he'd said.

She shook herself angrily. She was not going to ruin

this lovely evening by going over and over all that, she thought. It would be a total waste of her emotional energy, and she'd wasted enough of that already.

As she wandered up the gently sloping terrain, she wondered if Benjamin and Rosie would be around somewhere, but so far there'd been no sign of them. Helena smiled to herself; this had been the perfect place for Benjamin, Helena thought, as Isobel had known it would be. And when he and Louise were eventually told that their futures were secure—because Oscar and his wife would obviously be keeping them on—they would be over the moon. Mulberry Court would still be owned—and partly lived in—by the Theotokis family.

As she strolled on, her mind a kaleidoscope of shifting thoughts, Helena found herself at the very top of the grounds which would then lead her down the winding path towards the willow tree. She realized that for some unknown reason she hadn't gone there at all since being here all these weeks. It hadn't been a deliberate thing, more a subconscious wish to leave certain memories alone, she thought briefly. To peer inside the lowering branches might seem like opening a tomb…

So what was dragging her feet towards the tree? she asked herself now as, presently, there it was, its graceful branches reaching the ground, almost still in the light breeze. With an overpowering sense of resignation, Helena knew she was going to go in and sit on that flat tree stump just one more time. *Confront the problem*—she could hear her father's voice—*confronting a problem is halfway to solving it.*

Well, Helena knew she wasn't going to solve this particular problem—the problem of loving someone who loved someone else—but here goes, she thought, as she parted the branches of the tree and entered into the sweet, damp darkness…

It was about half an hour later that she heard his voice and, with her eyes still closed, Helena smiled. She wasn't asleep, she told herself, only daydreaming as she'd been sitting there surrounded by all the gentle, friendly ghosts of her past. She could hear them whispering, telling secrets, laughing…

'Heleena…' The voice, only slightly louder now—but she was not going to open her eyes. This was a mesmerising event…one which would never happen again. Hold on to the daydream, she told herself. Hold on to it…

He had been gazing down at her for some time, drinking in her appearance, She looked so childlike, so naïve, making the years between somehow melt away…

Then, 'I knew this is where I would find you.'

Suddenly, jerked from her semi-consciousness, Helena's eyes shot open and she stared up into Oscar's deep, penetrating gaze. For a full five seconds she didn't know whether she was awake, asleep or somewhere in between, but then he moved towards her, holding out his hands to raise her up, gathering her into his arms, crushing her to him, making her gasp. She *was* awake! This was real!

Saying no more, Oscar's lips found her mouth, her neck, the smooth skin of her bare shoulders—then her mouth once more, deeply, longingly, as if he were quenching his thirst with a draught of pure nectar. 'Heleena,' was all he murmured again.

And, clinging to him, Helena knew she wasn't going to let him go. It was the final curtain on this particular act in her life—this must last her for ever! With her arms raised and her hands entwined in the thickness of his hair, she leaned into him, her head dropping backwards, her trembling lips parting to receive his manly, seductive touch, and the feel of him, the smell of him, made her world revolve in crazy circles...round and round, making her feel so dizzy that if he hadn't been holding her closely she would have sunk to her knees on the ground.

Then, suddenly, abruptly, Helena's principles returned and reluctantly she pulled herself away and stared up at him in total confusion and dismay. What *was* this? she asked herself. What was he making her do? What was she allowing him to do?

'Oscar—' she said shakily '—this...this isn't right... is it?'

Still holding her, he murmured, 'It feels exactly right to me, Helena.'

'But—Allegra?'

He frowned down at her. 'Allegra?'

'Well...I'm assuming that she's the wife you'll be bringing here in the not too distant future,' Helena began, and he interrupted her.

'Allegra Papadopoulos—and her sister Callidora— are old family friends,' he said. 'Nothing more. Allegra is like the kid sister I never had.'

'But...her baby?' Helena said. 'The baby she lost...?'

'Helena, Allegra's baby is absolutely nothing to do with me,' Oscar asserted firmly. He paused. 'Allegra is a rather...unusual...woman. She has no wish to be married, but is determined to produce a child.' He shrugged. 'In my view, every child does better with two parents, if possible. But Allegra's always been terribly headstrong. She'll probably get her way in the end.'

Helena swallowed, for some reason feeling glad that Allegra would not be the wife Oscar intended bringing here, but—did it matter which woman became his wife?

There was silence for a few moments after that, while Helena tried to make sense of this situation. Then, thinking that perhaps his need for her at this moment was more to do with his raw grief following his father's death, she said, 'I hope all the arrangements in Greece went ahead without too many problems, Oscar...' After all, she thought, people usually liked to talk about life-changing events in their lives. He let her go slightly and looked down into her eyes.

'There are other, rather more important things, that are my concern now,' he said.

Helena steeled herself. 'About the house, you mean—and bringing your wife here?' she began but, before she could say another word, he had dragged her back towards him roughly, their faces so close that she could feel his rapid breath fanning her cheek.

'Yes, it is about my wife—or my prospective wife,' he said evenly. 'And I'm hoping you can help me out with that.'

She could help him out! How? And why?

'You'll have to give me a clue as to how I can possibly be of assistance,' she said, hearing her voice tremble as she uttered the words.

'I did give you a clue the night we came back from Greece,' he said, but unfortunately you didn't pick up on my perhaps clumsy hint.'

'Clue? What clue?' Helena asked, totally mystified. He was talking in riddles!

Then, after the longest moment of her life, Helena heard Oscar say the words she'd thought were lost to her for ever.

'It is *you* that I love, *Heleena*,' he said quietly. '*You* are the wife I was talking about…you are the only woman I would ever want to marry… Didn't you realize…?'

Almost swooning with amazement, Helena looked up at him. How was she supposed to have realized it? 'Well, that wasn't exactly what you implied on that night,' she said. 'You must think I am so stupid!'

Holding her so closely that they might have been one person, he whispered, 'You are not stupid, *Heleena*…. you are the sweet, intelligent, innocent girl that I have always known, have always loved. You are the girl who has made me unable to accept anyone else, to commit to anyone else. You are the woman I have been waiting for.' He rested his mouth on top of her head for a moment. 'Before we met again, I'd convinced myself that I would never marry—because no one else would ever do. And now…' he held her away from him gently '…I have to make you see, make you understand why I was forced to walk away from you—from us—all that time ago. And make you say that you will marry me… marry me soon…*kopella mou…*'

CHAPTER TWELVE

HAND in hand and saying very little, they made their way back to the house, Helena feeling almost drunk, delirious with happiness. She knew that her colourful imagination went to extreme lengths at times, but today went beyond anything her dreamy mind could come up with. This was paradise. Somewhere, quietly in the background, her guardian angel had been at work.

As they let themselves into the silent house, Oscar led Helena into the conservatory, closing the door behind them. They didn't bother to switch on the lamps; the silver beams from a pale moon was enough to infiltrate the corners, to light up the shadows of the room.

Feeling as if her knees were not going to be able to hold her up for much longer, Helena sat down on the long sofa and looked up at Oscar. He had gone across to gaze out of the window and now he half-turned towards her, the strong profile, the determined jaw testament to his powerful bearing, his superiority in any situation he found himself in. Helena shivered with sensuous pleasure. This was the man who'd always been the love of her life, and he had just told her that he wanted to marry her! And that he *loved* her!

But first he must tell her. She *had* to know.

'Why did you abandon me all that time ago, Oscar? Why didn't you tell me what I had done wrong?' she whispered. 'Why did you stop loving me?'

Now he turned towards her, his expression ominous in its intensity. 'I have never stopped loving you! And you had done *nothing* wrong, *Heleena*! You could, would never do anything wrong!' He ran a hand through his hair restlessly. Then, choosing his words...

'It all happened during the time of our last vacation here...just before you were going off to university,' he said slowly. 'Two dreadful, unimaginable things occurred at the same time and I was called back home urgently.' He paused before going on. 'Our company was within a hair's breadth of total disaster, thanks to unforeseeable circumstances in the industry as a whole, the first such thing to happen in our long history and a total shock, I can tell you. We had to move fast because it was something which had to be dealt with quickly, and it was necessary for me to be there, to understand, almost at once to assume responsibility—to take my place at the head of the team.'

Helena listened without saying anything, realizing what a bombshell the prospect of failure must have been for the mighty Theotokis empire.

After a moment, Oscar went on, 'But much, much worse, at exactly that same time my poor father was diagnosed with a debilitating disease from which he had no hope of recovery.' Oscar swallowed. 'Only the prospect of slowly declining health. And my father was a very proud man. Before his illness he worked every single day of his life, he was an unstoppable, driving force and the prospect of becoming wheelchair-bound was something he could barely face, could barely tolerate.' Oscar shut his eyes against the memory of that hideous time, before going on. 'And he was emphatic that his condition should not be widely known; he didn't want the news to become public property, it would not have been good for the company. He didn't want people to know—and to pity him. To be pitied would have been the final straw.' Oscar shook his head slowly, the pain of that time still hurting him deeply. 'Of course, certain members of the company had to be told, but by various means and for a considerable time it was kept largely a secret until, eventually, that became impossible.'

Oscar turned to look down at Helena, and she could see from the agony in his eyes how much he had loved and respected his father, how much he had cared for the older man's predicament, and for the name of their illustrious company.

'So, there was no alternative; I had to put the rest of my life on hold and do my family duty,' Oscar went on heavily. 'I had so much to learn from my father—and to learn quickly while he still had the strength to instruct and advise me.'

Helena had listened to every word, knowing what it was costing Oscar to go over that painful time. But... 'Couldn't you have told me, Oscar? You know I would have understood,' she said. 'And I would have waited for you, however long it took. Didn't you know that?'

'How could I ask such a thing of an eighteen-year-old girl just about to go out into the world for the first time?' Oscar demanded. 'You would be meeting other people, other men; you deserved to have a life of your own without emotional responsibilities.' He hesitated. 'I knew my path was going to be long and onerous… How could I have held you back? Besides, I was under a vow of secrecy about my father's illness. I could tell no one, not even someone I knew I could trust.' Oscar heaved a long sigh. 'I gave my word, and I could not break that,' he said.

After a moment, Helena said, 'I found it so hard, Oscar, so terribly hard…I just couldn't understand…'

He interrupted her. 'And it was so hard for me, too!' he said harshly. 'Don't you think I was full of regret? Don't you think I felt bad? That not only was I losing you, but I couldn't tell you why!' Oscar's expression contorted at his own words. Then, 'I thought of you so much, *Heleena*…I thought of you all the time…I imagined you married to someone else, and that thought tormented me.' He sighed deeply. 'Until, finally, the pressures I was under forced me to think of nothing else but the task I was faced with.' He paused for a long moment before adding, with a trace of cynicism, 'And I can recommend relentless work, relentless routine, as a very effective antidote to the human need for love.'

Slowly, Helena got to her feet and went over to slide her arms around Oscar's neck, resting her head on his shoulder, and he immediately enfolded her in his arms. But of course she would have waited for him, she thought. Well, without realizing it, hadn't she been doing just that?

He gazed down at her, then kissed her closed eyelids tenderly.

'Must I go down on one knee to hear you say that

you will be my wife, *Heleena*?' he murmured, and she smiled.

'Oscar, you should have known the answer to that— and all you needed to do was to tell me that you still loved me,' she said.

Then, in the enveloping silence of the room, their lips met in a long, deeply sensuous kiss that took them back to those halcyon days, days which were not gone and forgotten...days which were to return.

Presently, gently pulling away, Helena said, 'I've got something I want to tell you, Oscar...something lovely...something amazing.' He raised one dark eyebrow as she continued. 'A few days ago, I found some letters—well, actually they found me.' She swallowed. 'What I mean is—I was meant to find them,' she added, 'and they were written from just after I'd left home to go to university, until the last week before my father's death.'

Helena struggled with her emotions for a moment, unable to continue, and Oscar frowned slightly.

'Go on,' he murmured.

'They were letters between Isobel and my father, Oscar, and they were left in very tidy date order. The first one was from Isobel, thanking him for some extra work she'd asked him to do, and then there was his reply to her. And this correspondence appears to have continued regularly until four years ago.' Now Helena couldn't stop her tears from sliding gently down her face. 'They are the most beautiful letters I have ever read of a slowly emerging love story between two people who surprise themselves by discovering that—later on in their lives, and quite unexpectedly—they have deep feelings for each other. And it obviously gave them pleasure to say all this by writing to each other about it.' Helena wiped her cheek with the back of her hand. 'And it's clear that, eventually, they...they did become lovers.' Helena dropped her voice, as if telling a secret.

If he was astounded at this news, Oscar gave no sign. But—why should he, why should anyone be surprised? His great-aunt had always been a beautiful and gracious woman, and Daniel Kingston an attractive and charming man who, despite having worked all his life on the land, had always had the manner of a rather gallant gentleman. Yes, they would have made perfect partners. And it should never be forgotten that intimate feelings were not the preserve of the young, Oscar thought. Love was for everyone, if you could find it.

'Where did you find the letters?' he asked softly.

Helena smiled briefly. 'In my room there is a chest of drawers which has a secret compartment. Only Isobel and I knew about that,' she said. 'And that's why I know that she wanted me to see the letters, she wanted to share them with me. She knew I'd find them one day.' Helena closed her eyes for a second. Then, 'I feel... ecstatic...that my wonderful dad found love a second time in his life, Oscar, and with a lady who'd meant so much to me, too.' She paused. 'I feel as if I'm having too much happiness all at once,' she said slowly.

It was quite late by the time they eventually decided to have supper and presently, in the kitchen, Oscar watched while Helena took the delicious food from the fridge, then carefully poured oil and vinegar and honey into a bowl to prepare a dressing for their salad. He loved watching the way she used her slim fingers, the way her pale forehead creased into the merest semblance of a frown as she bent over the task, the way her dark eyelashes fanned the curve of her cheek...

They ate the meal in comparative silence, both relishing the distinctive love-enhanced atmosphere in the room, the sense of emotional security that bound them. And every now and again their eyes would meet and a silent message would pass between them—a message which had hung, unspoken, for so long.

But Oscar knew that there were things he must say to Helena—to make sure that she understood that by marrying him, her life was never going to be the same again.

He took a deep breath, and looked across at her. 'Are you fully aware of how marrying me is going to change your life, Helena?' he asked. 'Are you...are you sure you are ready for it? Are you sure you can bear it?'

Helena looked at him steadily, a faint smile on her lips. 'When people commit to a relationship,' she said slowly, 'it usually does mean a complete change to their lives, doesn't it? Isn't that what both parties expect... and want?'

'Of course,' Oscar said, 'and it's certainly what I want! But I realize how far you've come from your childhood here, how hard you've worked to achieve the independence you've earned. Are you prepared to give that up?' His face was serious for a moment. 'Because, you see, I cannot give up *my* career. I will never be able to just walk away from my responsibilities, and it will mean that you, too, will be affected.' He reached across and covered Helena's hand with his own, holding her tightly, before going on.

'I have to be in Greece and travel elsewhere abroad at regular intervals—and you will need to be with me sometimes. I will need to introduce you as my wife, I mean, it'll be important for us to be together. Not all the time, of course,' he added quickly, 'and Mulberry Court would always be our English base—but we cannot be here as often as perhaps you would like, Helena,' he said. 'Some compromise will be needed.'

Helena's eyes swam with tenderness. Precious though Mulberry Court was, it could never be as precious as flesh and blood, she thought. Could never be compared with being in the company of someone you deeply, truly loved.

'But Oscar, wasn't that what Isobel did—all her life?' Helena asked. 'She made it work. She travelled with Paul and was often abroad with him—but still managed to keep a firm foothold here as well.' Helena smiled. 'It's going to be history repeating itself, isn't it—and what better example do we have to follow?' She paused. 'And if you're worrying about my career being cut short—well, I can help *you*, can't I? I'd really love to find out how you make the company work, what it entails…the secret of its success.'

Thoroughly enthused by this thought, Helena went on, 'I mean it, Oscar. It would be a complete change of scene for me—and I'd enjoy the challenge.' She smiled at him pertly. 'I do very well at interviews. I'm sure you would find me a suitable candidate for the post of your PA.'

Oscar looked across at her flushed features longingly. Then, 'There is something else that perhaps we should talk about,' he began, and Helena raised her eyebrows. What else could there be?

Oscar came straight to the point. 'I want us to have children...I mean I would *love* us to have children. Several children, to be a real, noisy family.' He paused. 'I've never heard you express an opinion on parenthood, but...'

'You mean...I would be expected to produce heirs for the family firm, to carry on the name?' Helena began, and he interrupted fiercely.

'Hell, *no!*' Oscar exclaimed, leaning closer and taking both of her hands in his. 'I want us to have children for *us*, to see them grow up happily—and for much of the time here, at Mulberry Court. To give them brothers and sisters, something that I never had.' He shrugged. 'And who knows? If we are lucky enough to produce children and one of them chooses to follow in the family footsteps—well, that'll be fine. But it won't be a pre-condition of being a Theotokis,' he added firmly. He paused, smiling briefly. 'And, anyway, I seem to remember that Isobel stated a wish that a couple with children might buy the house. So...we would be carrying out her instructions, wouldn't we?' he said.

Suddenly, the ensuing silence was broken by Helena's mobile ringing and, raising her eyes at Oscar, she picked it up to answer it. It was Louise and, after a few moments of brief conversation, Helena ended the call and stood up.

'Louise apologizes profusely for the lateness of the call,' Helena said, 'but wonders whether we would like to go down to the cottages for a celebratory nightcap.' She shrugged. 'I didn't realize it, but today is Benjamin's birthday,' she added.

It was past midnight before Oscar and Helena left the cottage and started strolling back to the house. It was a perfect evening, enriched by the early summer scents of honeysuckle, hawthorn and cow parsley. As Helena gazed upwards briefly, the stars in the night sky twinkled and shone seductively, matching the glow in her eyes. Oscar encircled Helena's waist tightly.

'Well,' he said, looking down at her, 'did you have any inkling about that?'

Helena smiled. 'Sort of,' she said, not really surprised at Benjamin's request that Mulberry Court might look after itself for a few days at the beginning of next month while he took Louise to London to show her the sights. And with a further request that he might bring his young children back for a short holiday in Dorset.

'Louise has heard me banging on about Andrew and Daisy for long enough; I think she deserves to see them for herself,' Benjamin had said, adding, 'I don't get many chances to bring them away for a holiday, and Mulberry Court is such a perfect place for children.'

Helena glanced up at Oscar. 'It's impossible not to see how close, more than close, Benjamin and Louise have become,' Helena said. 'And I think it's lovely for them, don't you?' She smiled quickly. 'Louise adores children, I do know that, and she's going to love having Benjamin's here for a holiday.' And after a moment Helena added, 'Wouldn't it be great if Louise and Benjamin got together, and really became a couple?'

'It would be perfect all round,' Oscar agreed. He

paused. 'Do you think that might have been one of Isobel's little plans?' he asked. 'She was always an incurable romantic.'

Helena smiled. 'I shouldn't be at all surprised,' she said. She looked away for a second, thinking what a very long, eventful day it had turned out to be. 'I notice that neither of us bothered to mention anything about the new owners who were going to be residing frequently at Mulberry Court,' she said. Oscar squeezed her waist more tightly.

'Tonight didn't seem the appropriate occasion,' he said. 'After all, we had spoken at length of my father's demise, and Louise had been so touchingly sympathetic, and, after that, we were enlightened about her and Benjamin's wish to spend time together, away from here, and about his children coming to stay...' Oscar paused... 'Of course, for obvious reasons, they are going to be thrilled and excited when we do tell them, but I thought our own personal announcement could wait.' He smiled down into Helena's upturned face. 'Because I want to savour it...to hold on to it for just us...for a little while longer,' he added.

They let themselves into the silent house and, as they passed the door to the library, Oscar instinctively led Helena inside and looked up at the portrait of his great-aunt.

'Aunt Isobel,' he said softly, 'what plots have you been hatching?'

Helena wandered over to the alcove which held her figurines, and glanced up at Oscar. 'You know, Oscar, the only things I ever imagined I would possess are these two beautiful lovers,' she said quietly. 'To be left so much else of value never even crossed my mind.'

Oscar was well aware of that. Helena was the most generous, unworldly woman he had ever met. And her night-time mumblings as she'd sleepwalked that night proved her own words.

Suddenly, something made Helena pause in her thoughts—something she'd been meaning to ask Oscar and had kept forgetting to do, and which she was past caring about now. But still… Without looking at him, she said, 'Who was the lady who turned up the other day—the lady with the children, Oscar?'

'Oh—that,' he said non-committally. He frowned briefly, as if trying to remember something, then went over to one of the shelves and took down the envelope he'd left on top of the books. Without a word, he handed it to Helena and, after hesitating for a second, she opened it slowly.

Inside was a handwritten letter and two brightly coloured childish pictures decorated with hearts and flowers and a big *'Thank You'* emblazoned on the front of them. The more formal one read:

Dear Mr Theotokis
What words are there, in any language, to ex-
press one's gratitude for the gift of life? You
may remember a dreadful road accident which
happened a few months ago to me and my fam-
ily while we were in the area on holiday. I later
learned that you were the person who rescued us
from almost certain death. Subsequently, we were
in hospital for a number of weeks, but thank-

fully, are fully recovered now. I have tried to contact you before this, but was told you live mainly abroad. We are able to return home to Italy now, but I do hope there is an opportunity for the children to meet you one day, to thank you properly for your swift and selfless action which saved our lives. But for now—I thank you, Mr Theotokis. I thank you from the bottom of my heart, and God bless you.

It was signed *'from Maria, Antonio and Paolo Giolitti'.*

Helena looked up with tears in her eyes but, before she could speak, Oscar said, 'Do you remember the night I was held up on my way to the Horseshoe Innn? That first weekend?'

Of course she remembered, and Helena felt a pang of true remorse. She'd thought his surly attitude that night had been because he was annoyed at being held up on his journey. Instead of that, something much, much more important had happened.

'So—tell me about it,' she said quietly.

Oscar shrugged. 'It was pure chance that I was first on the scene,' he said casually. 'I saw them trapped in the back of the car, which had landed on its side...so I ran across and managed to get them out...the doors were jammed so I had to smash the window.'

Helena shuddered as she pictured the scene, hating herself for her ungenerous thoughts at the time. And when the woman and children had turned up here at the house, she'd thought the very worst of him then, too. How wrong could you be? she thought. Jumping to conclusions was a dangerous thing to do.

Carefully, Helena tucked the letters back into the large envelope and replaced it on the bookshelf. 'I had…wondered…whether those beautiful boys might have been yours, Oscar,' she admitted quietly.

He smiled down at her. 'I don't have any children,' he said, adding darkly, 'Not yet.'

They made their way upstairs together and, without hesitation, Oscar guided Helena into his bedroom and closed the door firmly. Without putting on the lights, he took her hand and they wandered across to gaze out of the window, the peace of the beautiful surroundings matching the peace in both their hearts—the peace of knowing that something longed for had happened, had come true at last.

Then he put his arms around her in a close embrace and Helena leaned her head into his neck, loving the feel of him, loving the familiar, sensuous smell of his warm skin. She turned her head slowly to gaze up at Oscar, nestling into him, her soft curves melding with the masculine strength of his frame. She raised her hand, tracing the contours of his face, touching his lips gently with her forefinger, which he immediately took between his teeth. Then, 'Do we have to…I mean is it necessary for us to be married in Greece?' she asked tentatively. 'It's just that I would really love to…'

He interrupted her, his dark eyes burning deeply into hers. 'We shall be married wherever you like, Helena. Just so long as it's soon.'

'Then I would like it to be here, in the garden at Mulberry Court…with just a few of us. Of course we would go to Greece afterwards for an appropriate ceremony, do whatever protocol demands—that would only be fair...' Her words came quickly, and Oscar hushed her gently.

'That's a minor detail,' he assured her, 'which will be dealt with as necessary.' He paused. 'And I, too, would like the ceremony to be held here, with just the people we love—past and present—to hear us make our vows.'

And in her dreamy mind's eye Helena could already see it. She would be wearing a simple white cotton dress, trimmed with lace, and there would be a single white rose in her hair and a spray of similar flowers in her hand. And the modest expense would be settled with her father's legacy. The money she had been keeping for something very, very special.

For several moments they remained there locked together, without speaking, and Helena could only marvel at the surging tide of happiness that rippled through her entire body, painting her cheeks with a rosy warmth, sending a delightful tingle right down her spine to her toes. She shuddered slightly, pleasurably, and Oscar looked down at her, his expression telling her everything she'd ever wanted to know. Then he lowered his head to kiss her, pulling her gently even closer, and Helena clasped her arms around his neck and closed her eyes, her lips very slightly parted to receive his kiss. A kiss so soft yet so passionate, so all consuming.

Then, with his perfect timing, Oscar led her over to the bed and they both sat down, and Helena leant forward to slip off her sandals, conscious that he was unzipping her dress, releasing her bra...

He laid her down gently and took his place beside her, and Helena turned her head to gaze into his eyes, those black, impenetrable eyes which had haunted her memory for so long.

'As to the matter you mentioned a little while ago, Oscar,' she murmured, 'I think—perhaps two of each— if you're happy with that?'

He smiled at her darkly. 'Perfect…to start with,' he agreed. 'And since there's no time like the present, *ko-pella mou*—tonight, we shall make a beginning.'

* * * * *

Mills & Boon® Hardback

March 2012

ROMANCE

Roccanti's Marriage Revenge	Lynne Graham
The Devil and Miss Jones	Kate Walker
Sheikh Without a Heart	Sandra Marton
Savas's Wildcat	Anne McAllister
The Argentinian's Solace	Susan Stephens
A Wicked Persuasion	Catherine George
Girl on a Diamond Pedestal	Maisey Yates
The Theotokis Inheritance	Susanne James
The Good, the Bad and the Wild	Heidi Rice
The Ex Who Hired Her	Kate Hardy
A Bride for the Island Prince	Rebecca Winters
Pregnant with the Prince's Child	Raye Morgan
The Nanny and the Boss's Twins	Barbara McMahon
Once a Cowboy...	Patricia Thayer
Mr Right at the Wrong Time	Nikki Logan
When Chocolate Is Not Enough...	Nina Harrington
Sydney Harbour Hospital: Luca's Bad Girl	Amy Andrews
Falling for the Sheikh She Shouldn't	Fiona McArthur

HISTORICAL

Untamed Rogue, Scandalous Mistress	Bronwyn Scott
Honourable Doctor, Improper Arrangement	Mary Nichols
The Earl Plays With Fire	Isabelle Goddard
His Border Bride	Blythe Gifford

MEDICAL

Dr Cinderella's Midnight Fling	Kate Hardy
Brought Together by Baby	Margaret McDonagh
The Firebrand Who Unlocked His Heart	Anne Fraser
One Month to Become a Mum	Louisa George

Mills & Boon® Large Print
March 2012

ROMANCE

The Power of Vasilii	Penny Jordan
The Real Rio D'Aquila	Sandra Marton
A Shameful Consequence	Carol Marinelli
A Dangerous Infatuation	Chantelle Shaw
How a Cowboy Stole Her Heart	Donna Alward
Tall, Dark, Texas Ranger	Patricia Thayer
The Boy is Back in Town	Nina Harrington
Just An Ordinary Girl?	Jackie Braun

HISTORICAL

The Lady Gambles	Carole Mortimer
Lady Rosabella's Ruse	Ann Lethbridge
The Viscount's Scandalous Return	Anne Ashley
The Viking's Touch	Joanna Fulford

MEDICAL

Cort Mason – Dr Delectable	Carol Marinelli
Survival Guide to Dating Your Boss	Fiona McArthur
Return of the Maverick	Sue MacKay
It Started with a Pregnancy	Scarlet Wilson
Italian Doctor, No Strings Attached	Kate Hardy
Miracle Times Two	Josie Metcalfe

ROMANCE

A Deal at the Altar	Lynne Graham
Return of the Moralis Wife	Jacqueline Baird
Gianni's Pride	Kim Lawrence
Undone by his Touch	Annie West
The Legend of de Marco	Abby Green
Stepping out of the Shadows	Robyn Donald
Deserving of his Diamonds?	Melanie Milburne
Girl Behind the Scandalous Reputation	Michelle Conder
Redemption of a Hollywood Starlet	Kimberly Lang
Cracking the Dating Code	Kelly Hunter
The Cattle King's Bride	Margaret Way
Inherited: Expectant Cinderella	Myrna Mackenzie
The Man Who Saw Her Beauty	Michelle Douglas
The Last Real Cowboy	Donna Alward
New York's Finest Rebel	Trish Wylie
The Fiancée Fiasco	Jackie Braun
Sydney Harbour Hospital: Tom's Redemption	Fiona Lowe
Summer With A French Surgeon	Margaret Barker

HISTORICAL

Dangerous Lord, Innocent Governess	Christine Merrill
Captured for the Captain's Pleasure	Ann Lethbridge
Brushed by Scandal	Gail Whitiker
Lord Libertine	Gail Ranstrom

MEDICAL

Georgie's Big Greek Wedding?	Emily Forbes
The Nurse's Not-So-Secret Scandal	Wendy S. Marcus
Dr Right All Along	Joanna Neil
Doctor on Her Doorstep	Annie Claydon

Mills & Boon® Large Print

April 2012

ROMANCE

Jewel in His Crown	Lynne Graham
The Man Every Woman Wants	Miranda Lee
Once a Ferrara Wife...	Sarah Morgan
Not Fit for a King?	Jane Porter
Snowbound with Her Hero	Rebecca Winters
Flirting with Italian	Liz Fielding
Firefighter Under the Mistletoe	Melissa McClone
The Tycoon Who Healed Her Heart	Melissa James

HISTORICAL

The Lady Forfeits	Carole Mortimer
Valiant Soldier, Beautiful Enemy	Diane Gaston
Winning the War Hero's Heart	Mary Nichols
Hostage Bride	Anne Herries

MEDICAL

Breaking Her No-Dates Rule	Emily Forbes
Waking Up With Dr Off-Limits	Amy Andrews
Tempted by Dr Daisy	Caroline Anderson
The Fiancée He Can't Forget	Caroline Anderson
A Cotswold Christmas Bride	Joanna Neil
All She Wants For Christmas	Annie Claydon